D0497782

Ten Years to Live

Ten Years to Live

Henry J. Schut

BAKER BOOK HOUSE
Grand Rapids, Michigan

Dedication

This book is dedicated to my brother, Dr. John W. Schut, whose dedication to the cause of finding a cure for ataxia has few parallels in the history of medicine. He wrote many articles on the cause and pathology of ataxia, that were published and quoted throughout the world.

Although he was unable to find a cure before the disease claimed his life at a relatively young age, his contributions to the work of medical research in the area of ataxia will stand for years to come as a monument to his dedication.

Contents

Preface

Appreciation

Introduction

One / A Happy Home 13

Two / The Shadow Looms 19

Three / Death Claims Its Victim 30

Four / A Strong Mother Rebuilds Her Home 34

Five / A New Cloud on the Horizon 40

Six / The Fight Begins 46

Seven / The Hurts of Social Stigma 54

Eight / Struggling for an Education 61

Nine / Seeking to Know God's Will 70

Ten / To Die Is Gain 77

Eleven / The Fight Intensifies 81

Twelve / Ataxia Marches On 89

Thirteen / "Why Me, O God?" 95

Fourteen / One Man's Fight 102

Fifteen / Time Is Running Out 109

Sixteen / What's the Use of Fighting? 120

Seventeen / Had God Answered Our Prayers? 126

Eighteen / "I'm Not Licked Yet" 130

Nineteen / Why Does He Want to Live? 139

Twenty / God Leads His Dear Children Along 147

Epilogue 151

Appendices 155

Preface

This is the true story of one family's struggle with ataxia, a hereditary disease that claimed one-half of its number for five generations.

It tells how men and women faced years of inevitable helplessness and death. It tells of the feelings of young people who watched and prayed as they waited apprehensively for the early symptoms of the disease. It tells of the mixed feelings of those who were spared—gratitude for themselves, but heartache as they saw brothers, sisters, and cousins die inches at a time. It relates how hopes were raised as new medications were tried and as different doctors searched for possible causes and cures— only to have these hopes shattered.

It tells of the men and women who married these unfortunate people, how they saw their mates and then many of their children succumb to this disease. It relates how they asked the soul-searching question, "Why, God, must they suffer so?" It describes how their faith in a loving and caring God was tested, how it at times wavered, and how it eventually triumphed over doubt.

Appreciation

My first expression of appreciation goes to my wife, Hazel, who patiently read each rough draft of this book and corrected the many errors that crept into the copy.

My thanks also to each of my children. To Dr. Lawrence Schut and Miss Linda Schut (R.N.) who helped me with the medical terms. To Darlene (Mrs. Ed Scott) who typed the final copy. To Marilyn and her husband, John N. Lee, for their constructive criticism. To Lois (Mrs. Charles Bakker) and to Wayne, for the encouragement they gave me to continue in the task.

My thanks also to Mrs. Patricia Winters, who typed the first draft and restructured many of the sentences.

I gratefully acknowledge and sincerely appreciate the time spent and the advice given by the Rev. LeRoy Koopman, who edited this book. Without his expertise I would not have been able to express the thoughts I wish to convey to the reader.

My thanks go, most of all, to my Lord—who helped me recall the many events of the past and gave me strength and comfort as I relived the heartaches and sorrows that have been so much a part of the life of our family.

Henry J. Schut

Introduction

Pa and I, clothed in heavy coats and boots, were ready to go to the barn and milk our eight cows. I was twelve years old and was expected to milk two or three of the easiest milking ones while Pa milked the others.

My mother was standing by the kitchen stove, preparing supper with her right hand, and balancing my five-month old brother Bill on her hip with the other.

Brother John, nearly three, was looking through a catalogue and occasionally exclaiming, "Mom, come here, see what I want!"

Sister Elsie, seven years old, was helping Mom by placing dishes on the table. The old Rayo kerosene lamp stood proudly in the middle of the table. It had been trimmed that morning and the glass chimney cleaned, so the flame shed a bright light throughout the room.

Brother Bert, who was ten, had found an old pair of Pa's shoes. He put his small feet in them and clumped across the floor.

Pa watched him for a minute. "Bert," he said, "they're a little big for you, aren't they?"

"Yes, they are now," said Mom, "but he will soon grow up and will be able to fill them."

Pa sat quietly and watched Bert for a moment. "That day I will never see."

Mom started to cry. She took the apron she was wearing and wiped the tears away. "You can't say that for sure, Pa. You don't know how long you may live yet."

Now I knew the answer to the questions I had wondered about so often. Why couldn't Pa walk very well? Why was it so hard at times to understand his talking? Why did he become so very sick whenever he had a cold? Why were his actions so different from those of the fathers of my friends?

I suddenly knew that Pa would not be with us very many more years, and that there probably wasn't anything any of us could do about it.

Though more than fifty years have passed since that memorable evening, every detail of the scene can still sweep vividly before me. Little did I know the role that this disease, hereditary ataxia, would play in my life and in the lives of everybody who was dear to me. That is what this story intends to tell. It is a true story, as best I can recall it.

1

A Happy Home

John Schut and Jennie Mol were married on February 14, 1908. Pa was thirty, and Mom was twenty-four. Pa must have had somewhat of an inferiority complex, because he said he never thought anyone could love him enough to marry him. He had some of those same feelings about God's love for him, because he did not make a commitment to Jesus Christ until he was thirty-two. I think that when he found out that someone like Mom could love him, he realized that surely God could love him too.

The year they married, Pa and Mom bought an eighty-acre farm about one and a half miles west of Silver Creek, Minnesota, about fifty miles northwest of Minneapolis. On the farm was a large T-type two-story house, which had to be one of the coldest in all of Minnesota. There was no insulation in the walls, no storm windows, no storm doors. On cold stormy winter nights ice formed in the tea kettle even though it was standing on the kitchen stove. All food that could not withstand freezing had to be stored in the small cellar beneath the house or put in the living room, where a large coal stove kept the temperature above freezing.

The living room furniture consisted of an old sofa, a couple of old wooden rocking chairs, and in later years an upholstered rocking chair which Pa used when he wore clean clothes—which was usually only on Sundays.

The barn was a wreck of a building, and in 1910 Pa replaced it with a new one. He added a hog house a year or so later. Besides these, the farm buildings consisted of a corn crib and a large granary. An old wooden windmill was centrally located and was used for pumping water, grinding feed, and sawing wood. Pa soon replaced this dilapidated structure with a new fifty-foot steel one. Since the wind didn't always blow, a large wooden storage tank stood near the barn. During the winter it was nearly covered with horse manure to help keep it from freezing. Even that didn't keep out the ice during the coldest weather, so we often had the cold job of lighting the wood in a partially submerged tank heater.

Water for the household was taken directly from the pump and carried into the house. One ten-gallon canful lasted through an ordinary day. On wash day or bath day, though, an additional supply had to be carried in. We had no flush toilets, which meant we had to go to an outhouse or use a container that was later carried outside. That task was never performed by volunteers.

Pa was a very strong man for his size, and he excelled most of his friends in any test of strength and endurance. I never knew him without a mustache. Mustaches were in style at the time, but Pa had one for a different reason. He had very crooked teeth, and he thought the mustache helped conceal them. In the winter the moisture from his breath sometimes formed icicles on the mustache, and he had to soak them off with hot water when he came into the house for meals. He was very sensitive about his person, and any critical comment made him angry.

Mom seldom took offense at anything. She not only tolerated his temper tirades, but by talking quietly to him helped him to get over them. Sometimes Pa put on the silent act and said very little. Mom had the patience and sense to wait until suddenly he would say, "I've been so angry for the last while." Then he would tell her about it and the silent treatment was over. Mom was about medium build with beautiful facial features, a firm mouth, and warm blue eyes. She loved everybody and was loved by everybody in return. Our home was open to friends, relatives, and the homeless. The food was plain but always enough, and we were ready to share whatever we had with anyone who stepped inside our door.

Less than a year after their marriage, the family doctor came to our home on a horse-drawn sled. One of my mother's aunts was also present to help deliver a child. The birth was a difficult one, and my brother was dead at birth. A small coffin was purchased and his body laid to rest in Lakeview Cemetery in Silver Creek Township. We still have the small metal plate inscribed with "Our Darling." Such plates were often attached to children's coffins in those days, then taken off at burial.

About a year and a half later, on June 5, 1910 at 10 P.M. (so I was told) I, Henry J., arrived. This birth was different. I couldn't wait until the doctor from Annandale, a distance of nine miles, got to our home by horse and buggy, and I made my way into the world as the doctor was driving on the yard.

Nearly two years later brother Bert J. appeared on the scene. He was born prematurely and was small at birth, but it didn't take him long to catch up. He was climbing chairs and walking in nine months. When we got into mischief it was usually his idea (but I was an eager accomplice).

I can't recall much of my life until I was four years old. I do remember that Pa often took me on his lap and taught me the capital letters of the alphabet by showing them to me in the old Dutch Bible. We were taught to speak the

Dutch language, as Pa and Mom spoke it most of the time in our home. They both had been born in America and had gone to English schools, but their friends and relatives spoke only Dutch. My grandparents had emigrated from Holland in the 1860s and 1870s. They had not attended school in America; and because they had settled in predominantly Dutch communities they had never learned to speak the English language very fluently. We learned very little English until we went to school.

Pa and Mom followed the strict custom of praying before each meal, reading a chapter from the Dutch Bible after the meal, and then closing in prayer. The prayers were always silent unless we had a visitor who was willing to pray audibly; then Pa asked him to pray. I use the pronoun "him" advisedly; a female was not expected to pray aloud. You can be sure we closed our eyes, because Pa occasionally checked during the prayer. If he caught us gazing around we spent several minutes of "make up" time. During the reading of the Bible we were compelled to listen intently because we never knew when he would stop and ask, "What was the last word I read?" When we were older we stood beside him and followed along as he read. We were usually expected to read the last verse. This custom taught us how to read, write, and speak the Dutch language. It also taught us all to respect both the Word of God and the deep religious heritage that Pa and Mom had in turn received from their parents.

We had our times of anguish too. One time Bert, who was always trying something new, pushed a navy bean up his nose. It really didn't bother him much at first, but after a time the moisture in his nostril caused the bean to swell and then the fun was over. Pa tried different tools to get the bean out, but to no avail. By this time I was crying as loudly as Bert. Pa then came up with an idea that I thought was brilliant. He put his mouth over Bert's open mouth, closed the open nostril with his finger and blew a quick strong breath into his mouth. The bean flew out on the floor.

One cold February morning when I was nearly five years old, Pa hustled Bert and me over to the neighbors without giving an explanation. Late in the day Pa came to get us and told us why: we had a new sister. Elsie was the only sister we had and we loved her dearly. She wasn't as prone by nature to get into mischief as her brothers, but she soon learned that if she was to retain any self-respect she would have to stand up for her rights.

One of the highlights of our week was attending the service at the Dutch church in the country. The full name of the denomination was the Reformed Church in America, but since almost all of its members were of Dutch descent most people simply called it the Dutch church. The services were usually held in the afternoon. We harnessed up the team of horses to our two-seater buggy for the forty-five-minute drive. The church owned a barn that accommodated about twenty teams, and the doors were large enough so we could lead them through without separating them. Each family could rent a stall for two dollars per year, which took care of the maintenance. By the time the men had taken care of the horses and sat down in the church, the church smelled more like a horse barn than a church, but everybody smelled alike so no one noticed. Even the minister had a horse, a cow, and about fifty chickens for which the church members provided feed and pasture.

Our church had three sections of pews. The custom was that the men sat on one side, and the women and children sat on the other side. The families who wanted to sit together sat in the middle section. Pa insisted on sitting with his family in the middle.

The Dutch psalms had a very slow tempo, and all the singing was done while the congregation was seated. By the time the sermon was to be preached I was often fast asleep.

I can recall a very deep sense of security as I put my head on Pa's lap and he put his arm around me. Since the sermons were about an hour long, I usually had a good nap.

In the cold and snow of winter, we rode on a heavy sled with a wagon box on it. Pa drove the horses while Mom and we children sat on a bed of straw covered to our noses with fur robes and blankets. The hour-long trip wasn't boring, as we played games and wrestled most of the way. But sitting in church was uncomfortable in winter weather. The single large register in the floor over a large wood furnace in the cellar could not conduct sufficient heat.

After the church service we would go to Grandpa Mol's home, about a block from the church, for coffee and cake. This was great fun as all of our cousins were there too—and Schut cousins were never in short supply.

Since we had no radios or television sets, we saw or heard little from the outside world, nor did we go very far from home. But we did enjoy the security of a home and of parents who loved us and each other.

2

The Shadow Looms

Since much of this story is about our immediate family and our cousins, I ought to pause and make some introductions. You may not believe this, but there were three sets of Schut cousins who had the same grandparents. You see, three Schut brothers married three Mol sisters, which meant we cousins were related through both our fathers and our mothers.

First, there was my own mother and father, Jennie Mol and John Schut, and their five children; the three I have already mentioned—Bert, Henry (me), Elsie—and the later arrivals, John Jr. and William.

Then there was my Uncle William Schut and Aunt Artie Mol, who had (from oldest to youngest) Alice, Bert, Henry, James, and Wilmena.

The third Schut-Mol combination was the Rev. Henry Schut and Bertha Mol, who had two children, Harold and Wilbert. Uncle Henry Schut spent most of his ministry in northwest Iowa, so we did not get to see them very much.

But with Uncle William and Aunt Artie and their family it was different. They owned a farm three miles west of ours and their children were in the same age range as we were. We saw each other at least once a week, and our lives were very much intertwined from the beginning.

You may have noticed in the introductions that the oldest boys of Uncle Will and Aunt Artie were named Bert and Henry, while the two oldest boys of my parents were named Henry and Bert. Strange, yes—but there was a reason for it. It was a very common practice among parents of Dutch descent to give their children the same names as their respective grandparents. Since our mothers were sisters and our fathers were brothers, the result was the same names for the first two boys. Although we could understand the custom, it didn't help us to know who was to answer when someone called for Henry or Bert. We solved it by adding an initial after our names. Since my father's name was John, I was called Henry J. and my brother was called Bert J. Since my uncle's name was William, my cousins were called Henry W. and Bert W.

We spent a lot of time together, Alice, we two Henrys, and the two Berts. Our fathers assisted each other in farm work, and life was pleasant.

But clouds were on the horizon. We noticed that Uncle Will began to be sick quite often. Then he began to stagger when he walked, and even his speech became difficult to understand. From time to time he would spend a week or so in bed, and he would cough and gasp terribly. Many times Pa and Mom had to help with the farm work.

It was during this time that we children began to hear snatches of conversation about a strange disease that was in our family line. People in other families didn't get the same kind of ailment Uncle Will had.

Our Grandmother Schut had gotten the disease, and she had died of it. So had many of my father's brothers and sisters. His sister Carrie Schut De Kraai had died of the disease and left three children. His older brother Gerrit had left nine children when he died, and his sister Allie Schut Klomp had left six children.

We never heard of anyone ever being cured of the disease. They always died. It took ten years after the first symptoms began to appear—sometimes more, sometimes less—but the result was always the same. The victims usually began to show the symptoms when they were about twenty-five years old. Gradually they became more and more disabled until they were not able to walk or talk. Finally, when they contracted a bad cold or pneumonia, they choked to death. It wasn't pleasant to think about.

During this time, when I was about five years old, my Uncle Henry and Aunt Bertha came for a visit. He was at that time serving a church in northwest Iowa. The three brothers and three sisters were deeply troubled at Uncle Will's illness, and Uncle Henry suspected that all was not well with his own body. My father was seemingly strong, yet he and Mom were very deeply concerned. After all, two of his older sisters and a brother had already died of the disease, and now it seemed certain that Uncle Will and Uncle Henry were also victims.

"There seems but one place to go," said Uncle Henry. "The Mayo brothers, in Rochester, Minnesota, are world-famous. If help can be found, we will find it there."

The three brothers took the train to Rochester, went through the clinic, and had a thorough examination. The doctors were convinced that Uncle Will had a nervous disorder, but they could find no cause for concern for Pa or Uncle Henry. That three others of the family had died of a similar disorder did not arouse enough interest in the doctors to motivate them to investigate any further. They suggested that it would probably die out in another generation or two.

The brothers came home with very little hope. They simply decided to permit God to work His will in their lives.

Uncle Will became progressively worse. In the winter of 1917-18, he contracted influenza, the plague which killed twenty million people worldwide. He died on January 1, 1918, at the age of thirty-three. It was a tragic loss, as it left Aunt Artie with four children and pregnant with the fifth. She was fortunate in being able to hire a cousin, who was single, to work the farm for her.

My Uncle Henry died of influenza on December 24 of that year. His earlier suspicions were correct; he too, had become a victim of the family disease. He had, however, been able to continue his preaching even though he needed a cane to walk. He was spared much of the disability of the disease because the flu shortened his life by several years. My Aunt Bertha was left homeless, with only a meager pension to provide for herself and her two sons. So she came to live with her parents, my Grandpa and Grandma Mol. Now two of the three Mol sisters were widows.

The sad news continued to come in. In 1920, my Aunt Grace Schut Ernissee died after being disabled for several years, leaving eight children with her husband. My Aunt Hattie Schut Demotts also died that year at the age of forty-eight, leaving seven children. She also died of the influenza; but unlike the others she had shown no symptoms of the family disease.

By the end of 1920, my father had one living sister of the eight brothers and sisters he had once had. Only Aunt Nellie Schut Tubergen was well. She apparently would not get the disease since she was past the usual age of onset.

The experience of our family with the disease also brought other facts to light. One was that only the parents who had the disease could pass it on to their children. Unfortunately, most of them had a number of children before they knew whether or not they were going to be afflicted. In 1920, there were fifty-one first cousins on my father's side, thirty-seven of whom had a chance of being afflicted.

At this point it might be well to pause and answer a question frequently raised: Why did the couples who knew their disease was hereditary continue to have children?

For one thing, birth control methods at that time were

neither effective nor readily available. For another thing, most of those folks simply didn't know much about birth control. But more than that, they believed it was wrong. They felt that whether or not to have a child was a decision that rested with God. To even think that a child would not be wanted was wrong, and to use any means to obstruct God's will was unthinkable.

Although this philosophy did bring sorrow and tragedy into the family, it was also a tremendous source of strength. Mom never questioned the wisdom of God. That not only gave her strength but was an example that her children never forgot.

Although Pa was older than Uncle Will he was still strong and able to work hard. He was almost forty years old—nearly ten years past the normal deadline for the first appearance of the disease. My parents were very hopeful that Pa was going to make it.

But it was not to be.

Little by little the symptoms began to appear, first intermittently, then constantly. He fell and broke his ankle. He began to find it difficult to perform some of the little tasks of everyday living, such as tying his shoes and buttoning his shirt. Driving nails and writing his name became fumbling, laborious ordeals.

I was only ten years old at the time and not completely aware of the heartache he carried. But I did notice that he no longer sang the gospel songs he loved so much, nor did he have the hearty laugh that I had heard so often. Despite this I never heard him complain or fret about how life was treating him.

One night I climbed on his lap and asked him, "Are you tired, Pa?"

"Why do you always ask me if I'm tired?"

"You just sit here in the living room in your rocker and don't read or say anything," I answered.

He said nothing.

Distress and frustration became more and more a part of his life. Outbursts of temper became more frequent as the discase progressed. We were sometimes the object of his anger. Most often, however, he vented his anger on objects or animals. He could no longer react quickly enough to control machinery or work with animals, and he vented his frustration on them.

Pa and Mom decided that we should move to a smaller farm so the work would not be so pressing. In 1920, we moved to a forty-acre farm about three-fourths of a mile from my birthplace.

The smaller farm had an old barn located in a low spot. During the spring or after a heavy rain the space behind the milking stalls would have as much as a foot of water in it and soon it became a quagmire of thin mud. We needed knee boots to milk the cows. Pa found it very difficult to walk through it and would sometimes fall in the mud up to his armpits. If it wasn't too cold I would roll up my overalls and walk through the mess with bare feet.

These conditions were intolerable, and since there was no way the old barn could be fixed, Pa decided to build a new one. This added to the financial burden we were under, as we were beginning to feel the pinch of the farm depression of the 1920s. Added to that, my father's inability to do much of the normal work forced us to hire help.

One of the most difficult tasks for Pa was putting the harness on the horses—he could not carry the harness and walk at the same time. So brother Bert and I devised a way. We placed a box beside the horse in the stall. I climbed on it and threw the front part of the harness on the horse while Bert held the back part as high as he could. Then I took the back part from Bert and threw it on the rear part of the horse. We then fastened the buckles and snaps together so the harness would stay in place. It took us quite a while to get a team harnessed and hooked up to a piece of machinery. Pa directed us but always held on to something so he would not fall. At first he was able to operate the machine if we had the horses hooked up to it; but as he began to get worse I was able to do the work better than he could, even though I was small and only eleven years old. At the age of twelve I could operate most of the farm machinery. With Pa's direction and Bert's help we managed to get most of the work done on time.

Cultivating corn was done with a one-row walking cultivator. Two horses furnished the power. Four shovels were attached to two different movable frames, which were mounted on two wheels. These movable frames had handles on them by which the operator could control the shovels as he walked behind. The horses were guided by two leather lines extending from bits in their mouths around the shoulders of the operator. Pa could control the shovels as he walked behind but could not control the lines with his shoulders. If he let go of the handles he would fall headlong to the ground. We solved this problem by fastening a seat on the frame of the cultivator. Bert or I now could drive the horses, leaving Pa free to operate the shovels. It was a boring job, and if I didn't watch closely enough the horses would veer too far over to one side and I would hear an impatient "Watch your business" from Pa.

The former owner had permitted the pasture fences to deteriorate and the cows could easily barge through them into the crops. Pa and I mended them in many places, but Pa could not pull the wire as tight as was necessary. Consequently the cattle frequently broke out into the cornfield.

On one particular August afternoon the cows found a weak spot in the fence and soon most of them were in the cornfield eating the green corn. To Pa this was the "last straw." He became almost completely irrational. He went into the house, got his single-barrel shotgun and started in his staggering walk to "fix" those cows so they would never get out again. Mom tried to reason with him, and although she was usually able to do so, this time she could not calm him down.

Pa walked out to the cornfield and started shooting at the cows. Fortunately the same disability that made it difficult for him to control his walking also made him a poor shot, so he wounded only one cow on the rear hip. Meanwhile Mom had phoned our neighbor across the road, my Uncle Will De Kraai. His oldest son, Ed (who later became a victim of the disease), came running over and met Pa as he was coming back from his shooting spree.

"Do you think that this is the way a Christian should act?" yelled Ed.

"No," said Pa. "I guess I just lost control of myself." He gave the gun to Ed and they walked home together.

I later helped Pa dress the wound on the cow's hip and it healed quickly.

The incident left an indelible impression on me. Even more noteworthy than Pa's temper was Mom's reaction to it. She never brought up the incident again. I was amazed how she accepted Pa without any reservations. Never did she criticize him before us, nor did she ever allow us to do so. My own reactions were mixed. I don't recall being afraid of Pa, but I often felt he was very impulsive and made unfair and hasty decisions. Yet I never lost my love and respect for him.

There was no windmill on this farm, so we had a one-cylinder Stover engine that drove a pump jack by means of a belt. This temperamental engine frequently refused to start. Pa was not a mechanic, and if the engine would not start he would not search for a reason. Instead he kept cranking until either he was completely exhausted or his temper caused him to stalk out of the pumphouse in a rage.

On one of these occasions, he encountered Mom a short distance from the pumphouse door. She walked up to him and calmly asked him not to be so angry. This angered him even more, and he picked up a stone. I thought he was going to throw it at Mom, but she calmly walked up to him, put her hands on his shoulders and looked him straight in the eyes. "Please, Pa."

He suddenly broke down and cried.

(Shortly afterward I got the engine started, which only needed a nut tightened on one of the dry cell batteries.)

By today's standards Pa and Mom had very little education. Pa went through the fifth grade and Mom finished the seventh grade. But they wanted their children to have what they had not received.

My school career began in a two-room country school about one and one-half miles from my birthplace, and about three-fourths of a mile from the second farm we moved to. I was small for my five years, and we had to walk both ways. If the weather was very cold and stormy Pa or one of the neighbors took us or picked us up, but that was the exception rather than the rule.

I soon found out that a small kid isn't very useful in a scrub baseball game, and that it's terribly traumatic, when sides are chosen up at recess and noon hours, to be picked after the girls have been chosen. So I shifted my energy to school work. I was able to excel in the academic area, passing the eighth grade exams before I was twelve. Pa was thrilled and wanted very much for me to go on to high school. But the high school was six miles away, and there was no way to get there every day. The few boys and girls who did go on to high school usually stayed in town and boarded in homes. On weekends they walked home. But we couldn't afford the cost, nor could Pa do the farm work without my help. There was to be no high school for me at that time.

Harvesting was always a busy time on the farm. It was exceptionally difficult for Pa as there was so much hand-work associated with it. A binder pulled by three horses cut the grain and bound it into bundles. Then it was our job to set up the bundles in shocks, about ten bundles to a shock. When the bundles were dry enough we hauled them on a rack and piled them in large stacks until a threshing machine could be hired. There was a technique in piling the bundles so the stacks would shed rain, and Pa had been an expert at it. Now he could no longer stand on the slippery bundles so Bert and I tried to throw the bundles where he could reach them while crawling on his hands and knees. As the stacks became higher I got on the stack, and Mom and Bert threw the bundles to me while Pa stood on a ladder and told me how to place them. It was a slow and tedious task, but we finished it.

One of the most difficult experiences for Pa was meeting people who did not know him, because he gave the impression that he was drunk. Our pump broke down one summer day, and Pa took one of my mother's uncles with him to get the part repaired. After having it repaired Pa put the pipe in the back seat of our 1919 Studebaker touring car. Being too long, it stuck out of the left side about two feet. On the way home he met a car. One of the lady occupants in the other touring car had her hand on one of the rods that held up the fabric roof. By freak chance the pipe that stuck out of Pa's car struck the diamond ring on the lady's finger, knocking out the diamond. Pa stopped.

As Pa started to walk toward the other car, the driver angrily shouted, "Drunk too, aren't you?"

Fortunately Mom's uncle could verify that Pa was sick, but the accident cost us $450 for a new diamond ring, an expense we could not afford. It turned out that the owner of the other car owned a grocery store in Minneapolis, so we paid the debt by shipping our eggs to him. He paid above market price and continued to be a steady customer after the debt was paid.

That accident and several other near accidents made it imperative that someone else learn to drive. Mom tried to learn but would panic whenever she was faced with a sudden decision. So, although I was only twelve, I was soon driving the old Studebaker. I couldn't reach the pedals, so a hard pillow was placed behind my back. By stretching my toes I could reach the clutch, the brake, and the gas pedal. We owned the car for ten years, and when we traded it off it had only eleven thousand miles on it.

As the disease progressed we noted a curious symptom that had been present in Uncle Will too. Pa seemed to sleep soundly, but between each breath he emitted a low moan. This was more noticeable if he was especially tired. He denied having any pain or even being aware of making any sound. We soon learned from other relatives that this was a definite characteristic of the disease and in some people was one of the first symptoms.

Life became a burden to my father. Walking and talking became more and more difficult. He resigned as deacon of the church because he was not able to walk well enough to take up the offering. Many people had trouble understanding him. But, he was determined to remain as active as possible.

3

Death Claims Its Victim

About three years after we moved to the small farm Pa
contracted pneumonia and became seriously ill. Since I
was thirteen and Bert eleven, we could do all the chores.

One day, on the way back from the mailbox, I picked a
four-leaf clover. In the house I showed it to Mom.

"I hope and pray that you will be fortunate throughout life," she said. Although little was said at home about
the disease, I knew what she meant.

Pa did recover from this attack, but his disability became worse with every cold.

During the summer of 1924, Pa thought that Bert and
I were old enough to take care of the old eighty-acre farm.
We began to prepare for the move by plowing the land in
the fall. One day in mid-September Pa went to the farm
with three horses and a riding plow we had bought, and
plowed all afternoon. The weather was cold with a light
rain, and Pa caught a severe cold. He was soon down in bed
with pneumonia. The doctor came and told us that he
doubted if Pa would survive this time. Hospitals were both
rare and far away, and the antibiotics of today were unknown, so it was up to the person's body to fight off the
illness. Apparently Pa had a premonition of his departure,
because he asked the local banker to come over and make
out his will. He wanted to make as many provisions as he

could, he said, so Mom could operate the farm business. He was by then unable to write, so he placed an X on the will. With the signature of two neighbors as witnesses the will became valid.

Pa was sick only four days, but the events of those days shaped much of my thinking and philosophy for life.

On the morning of the day of his death Pa asked for the Rev. Peter Siegers, our minister. He gladly came.

After reading from the Bible and saying a prayer, the minister asked Pa if he wished to say anything.

"Yes," said Pa, "I want to tell you about a dream I had just this morning."

"Please do," said Mr. Siegers.

It was difficult for the pastor to understand Pa, but Mom and I helped, as we were more accustomed to Pa's talking.

"Pastor," Pa said, "I dreamt that I was standing in the train depot, about to go on a journey. I had the ticket in my hand and the plans were certain. In fact, I could see the city to which I was going upon the horizon, and it was shining with splendor and light."

I had seen so many of Pa's angry outbursts that I had wondered at times how he could be like that and still be a Christian; but now I knew that God had revealed to him the certainty of his soul's destiny.

Soon after the minister left Pa asked Aunt Artie if she would sing "On Christ, the Solid Rock I Stand." With a broken voice she sang all the verses.

> My hope is built on nothing less
> Than Jesus' blood and righteousness;
> I dare not trust the sweetest frame,
> But wholly lean on Jesus' name.
>
> On Christ the solid rock I stand;
> All other ground is sinking sand.
> All other ground is sinking sand.

31

When darkness veils His lovely face;
I rest on His unchanging grace;
In ev'ry high and stormy gale,
My anchor holds within the vale.

His oath, His Covenant, His blood,
Support me in the whelming flood;
When all around my soul gives way,
He then is all my hope and stay.

When He shall come with trumpet sound,
O may I then in Him be found;
Dressed in His righteousness alone,
Faultless to stand before the throne.

Almost immediately after these words were sung, Pa lapsed into semiconsciousness.

About two o'clock in the afternoon he woke up and started to sing over and over again parts of the hymn "Guide Me, O Thou Great Jehovah." From other snatches of his delirious talk, we felt that he was reliving a choir rehearsal from his youth.

"Open wide the crystal fountain, whence the healing waters flow." He sang at the top of his voice, one syllable between each gasp of breath. "Strong Deliverer, be Thou still my strength and shield." Over and over again.

Several of our relatives and friends came to our home when they knew the end was near. Mom sat by the kitchen table, oblivious to the unwashed supper dishes. Several of our relatives sat around the room talking in subdued voices. The old kerosene lamp cast a dim yellow light throughout the room. The men were at Pa's bedside in the bedroom. Again and again we heard Pa's heavy breathing stop, and we thought he was gone. Then suddenly he would start to breathe again as his strong heart refused to stop.

Suddenly Mom put her head on the table and cried, "O Father, take him home so he won't need to suffer so much."

My Aunt Bertha remonstrated. "Jen, you may not pray for that."

"I don't know what else to pray for."

The prayer was answered within minutes. At about 9 P.M. on September 24, 1924, Pa went to be with the Lord, a sinner saved by grace.

The doctor told us later that the diaphragm had become entirely paralyzed. The mucus that should have been expelled by coughing continued to fill up the lungs until they could no longer take in oxygen. This was the manner in which most of the victims of the disease had died.

But really, he had begun to die many years before. Through the years a little part of his body died every day until the disease destroyed the means by which he took in the breath of life.

Now there were no more uncles or aunts who could die from the disease. Pa, Uncle Will, Aunt Allie, Uncle Henry, Aunt Grace, Uncle Gerrit, Aunt Carrie, Aunt Hattie—they were all dead. Only Aunt Nell, now forty-six, was alive. The next generation was not old enough to know who would live or who would die. And I was part of that generation. It was time to pray that somehow, in some way, God would help us find a cure before about half of the next generation—fifty-two of us in all—would begin to stumble and to speak with a slur.

4

A Strong Mother Rebuilds Her Home

Mom felt strongly that the father was designated by God to be the head of the home, but she was not a weak person. During the last years of Pa's life, when it was impossible for Pa even to write his name, she did most of the business at his direction.

Mom was always interested in other people, and their problems usually became her problems. She was called in many times when a baby was born, and to my knowledge never accepted payment for services.

Mom loved to visit and to have visitors, which sometimes meant that the house was not always in the neatest order. But true to her Dutch heritage she always kept it clean.

Mom could teach small Sunday school children or discuss theology with the minister. She was slow to criticize, but everybody knew what her convictions were and that they were not available for compromise. If she became angry she seldom showed it. We knew the behavior she expected. A few firm words of rebuke, if we digressed from this standard, were generally sufficient to keep us from pursuing our wayward paths.

All these characteristics helped our family to adjust to living without a father. Mom now had the responsibility for five of us. I was fourteen; Bert twelve; Elsie, nine; John four; and Bill, two. The responsibility of the day-to-day farm work fell on the shoulders of Bert and me. Fortunately we had been forced to accept much of this before Pa died.

It seemed to us that it would have been better to have stayed on the small farm, but Mom said, "Pa wanted us to move back to the home place, and we are going."

That ended the indecision, and the next spring we moved all of our stock and machinery back to my birthplace. Mom rented the land out to the neighbors for one year, and rented the small farm to a farmer who lived on it for one year. It was soon apparent that to rent out both farms was not a paying proposition. When a buyer came to buy the small farm, Mom sold it—even though it was for considerably less than we had invested in it. But it proved to be a wise decision as the farm economy continued to go down, and we would have lost both farms had we tried to keep them. Pa had mortgaged both farms to buy the small farm and build the new barn on it. By selling the small farm we were able to reduce the mortgage on the home place to a sum that we could handle.

In today's society we probably would have qualified for welfare or social security benefits. These, of course, did not exist, so it was a struggle to survive.

Mom seldom discussed the tragedy of Pa's death, but I knew there was a deep hurt in her heart and that she missed him very much. Although we were very poor and the future financial situation looked even worse, she had one of Pa's photos enlarged and placed in a beautiful wall frame. For a time I thought it was a very expensive luxury, but then I began to realize that I had not lost the dearest one in my life as she had. They had been married just seventeen years. Mom had several opportunities to marry again but never once considered it. Nor did her sisters,

Artie and Bertha, who were younger than Mom when their husbands died. They were "one man" women.

After renting out the farmland for one year Mom thought Bert and I could operate the land. We didn't know how much oats had to be sown to the acre, how much corn to plant to a hill, or hundreds of other things that a farmer must know to be successful. Fortunately we had helped Pa so much that we knew more than the average fifteen- and thirteen-year-olds did—but oh, the mistakes we made!

Planting corn required experience and skill. I had neither one, but I planted it anyway. The corn planter had a mechanism triggered by large knots on a wire stretched all the way across the field and held fast by stakes. The idea was that as each pair of rows was planted, the trigger on the planter would drop three or four kernels in a hill so that these kernels would also form a row crosswise to the direction of the planter. The stakes had to be moved to keep pace with the rows as they were planted, an act crucial for getting rows straight in the crosswise direction. The first year the rows were so crooked that we could not cultivate it crosswise at all. We tried hoeing by hand but soon found out that hoeing a field of twenty acres is an endless job. We had weedy corn that year! The next year I received a little training from a neighbor and the planting went much better.

I did most of the field work at first while Bert did most of the chores. We helped each other with the milking, and we argued at times about who was going to milk the hard-milking cows since all the milking was done by hand. The milk was then carried to the house where the cream was separated from the skim milk by a hand-operated separator. The cream was sold and the skim milk fed to the hogs.

It was amazing that things went as well as they did, and I still wonder how Mom endured all the mistakes we made.

She had confidence in us, I guess. Besides, she had very little time to spend directing us, as she had to care for our two younger brothers and Elsie.

Those years, however, were not unhappy. We spent much of our spare time visiting with Aunt Artie's family, and we had some wonderful times singing songs together, and playing all sorts of games. The disease that had killed our fathers was soon only a memory.

At sixteen or seventeen years of age I started to go to our church's young people's meetings. Christian Endeavor Society, as it was called, was attended by thirty or forty young people. It was the center of our social activities, and the place where boys met girls.

During the summer we used our old 1919 Studebaker to go to church. When winter set in, the roads became impassable for cars—which didn't matter much, because they wouldn't start anyway. There was no such thing as antifreeze in those days so we put the car on blocks and stored the battery in the cellar until spring.

Going to Christian Endeavor meetings with the horses wasn't such an unpleasant experience anyway. Quite often one of the neighbors took a team of horses and a bobsled with straw on the floor and lots of quilts, and picked up all the young people along the road. By the time we reached the church we had fifteen to twenty boys and girls in a three-foot by ten-foot box, which gave us a good reason to get close. It took an hour each way. If we didn't hurry the horses, it could take much longer.

One incident on one of those sleigh rides will bring back memories to anyone who lived in that era. Sleigh roads were made wherever the snow drifts were not so deep— which might be on the road, through the fields, over the lake, or through a thick woods. It was considered not only permissible but expected that anyone could start a sleigh road wherever it was most convenient. But during the spring thaw the sleigh roads might thaw unevenly. One evening our sleigh hit a slope of ice, lurched sideways, and threw us all against one side of the wagon box. Not designed to withstand fifteen people thrown against it, the whole side snapped off. All of us except the driver rolled out into the snow drift, rolling and tumbling over each other. Warm embraces were suddenly cooled off by snow on our faces, down our necks, under dresses, and in our hair. Several girls began crying, but they stopped as soon as they saw that the only damage was to the wagon box and to a few briefly interrupted romances.

Birthday anniversaries were often occasions for neighborhood parties. Some were by invitation, whereas others were "open house." Our home was open to these parties, even if we didn't have a birthday. Mom seldom discouraged this because then she knew where we were and what we were doing. Our kitchen was large and we could move the table to one corner and play many of the popular parlor games. We made our own music by singing songs such as "Skip to My Lou, My Darling." There were times, however, when Mom didn't appreciate the rough games we played— and not without reason, for many chairs and cups and saucers became the victims of our assault and battery.

When I was eighteen years old I had a sudden attack of appendicitis. I recovered quickly, but a month later, on a Sunday afternoon, I had a second attack. The doctor said the appendix should be removed by surgery but he thought it could wait until Monday morning. That decision nearly cost me my life.

By the time I was operated on at 10 A.M. on Monday, the appendix had burst and the poison had spread throughout my abdomen. The battle to save my life was on. There were no antibiotics or any of the other infection-fighting drugs, and I had to rely on my own body's defenses. The practice at that time was to keep patients in bed at least nine days after surgery. That practice caused a blood clot to form in my leg. Phlebitis set in, and pneumonia followed as the blood clot traveled to my lung. A huge abscess formed on one of my lungs and part of a rib was removed to provide better drainage. I was in bed for thirty-five days.

Very few people thought I would live; but they had not considered the power of my mother's prayers. She was by my bedside most of the time. One night after midnight I felt that I had reached the end of my endurance. Even with the many sedatives that were given, I was suffering intense pain. It seemed like I was at the bottom of a deep hole with only a small light coming in at the top. I tried to turn around, and as I did so I saw my mother on her knees beside my bed.

"O Lord, save my son," she sobbed.

I do not know how long she knelt there, but I am convinced that Mom prayed me out of the very gates of death.

5

A New Cloud on the Horizon

Aunt Artie was dearly loved by us all. She was about two years younger than Mom, shorter in stature, and somewhat heavier. She had a hearty laugh, which even with her many sorrows was heard often. Her face was rounder than Mom's, and the lines that grew in it were deeper. She had the same warm blue eyes that Mom had.

Aunt Artie possessed the same love for us all that Mom did, and we never doubted it. This love was the cement that held us together all of our lives. Yet Aunt Artie was more apt to let us know when she was angry. Usually there was a good reason, because when the ten of us came together it was a time that tried (wo)men's souls.

Alice, Aunt Artie's oldest daughter, was three years older than I, and the only girl in our clan until my sister Elsie came along. Alice was a little plumper than us boys, and we called her "foddy fatty." She had a quick temper, and we were experts at arousing it. Aunt Artie was watchful that we didn't carry the teasing too far, though, and with a sharp rebuke she would put an end to it.

Bert W. and I were the closest in age and we had many things in common. Bert W. was much more reserved and shy, yet his face broke into a smile very easily. He was a very persistent person and often spent hours working on a project or trying to make a machine work. He was a very kind and patient person, and I seldom heard him complain. He wasn't very interested in girls, as I was.

Henk (or Henkie, as he was sometimes called), the cousin with the same name as mine, was closest in age to my brother Bert J., and they spent a great deal of time together. Henk was full of vitality and prone to get into trouble—not of any major type, but enough to give his mother some anxious moments. His impulsive nature sometimes caused problems, yet he was quick to express regret for any difficulty he caused. Henk differed very much from his brother Bert W. in that it was very hard for him to accept any circumstances that were difficult or unpleasant. The four of us boys seldom quarreled, even though we worked and played together often.

Their brother Jim was several years younger than we were and closer to my sister Elsie's age. He was born with a self-confidence we didn't always appreciate. Jim was a born leader and sometimes we, who were older, didn't care to be led. He had a zest for life and loved any challenge that life held out to him. When he laughed he laughed all over, and so did everybody else.

Wilmena was born seven months after her father's death, when I was eight years old. She quickly became the sweetheart of us all. She was beautiful clear through, with a contagious smile and a twinkle in her eye. We called her "Kissy" because of her childhood habit of kissing everybody she knew.

My brother John was born two years after Wilmena, and my brother Bill was born two years later. They rounded out the Schut cousins of these two families. There were ten of us, from cousin Alice, the oldest, to my brother Bill, the youngest—a range of fifteen years. Often we were joined by Aunt Bertha's and Uncle Henry's two boys, Harold and

Wilbert, making nine boys and three girls of three families whose fathers were brothers and mothers were sisters.

Two of the few game boards we owned were a carrom board and a checkerboard. If our mothers had been given a choice, I'm sure they would have preferred to have us play those games more often. At least we were quiet and stayed sitting in one place for as much as an hour, a rarity for the boys. Because of the continuous motion and constant teasing and bantering, it was fortunate that our closest neighbors lived at a distance.

Aunt Artie owned an old organ and later a piano. No evening was complete until Alice sat at the piano and the rest of us sang. Aunt Artie's family was more musical than ours; our family tried to stay within a note or two of the correct ones. We especially loved to sing "When the Roll Is Called Up Yonder, I'll Be There." We firmly believed the words of this song. We were convinced that when that final roll was called we would indeed all be there. We had the assurance that although we were all sinners, we were "Saved by Grace," another hymn we often sang.

During this time, an incident took place that gave me another brush with death. One hot evening about fifteen of the boys in the community decided to go swimming. Since none of us owned bathing suits we waited until dark so we wouldn't be seen naked. We broke every safety rule of swimming—we didn't have pals and we swam in an area where there was a steep drop-off close to shore. Besides that, we had been warned by our parents not to swim in that lake or to go into the water after dark. I had never learned to swim so I stayed close to shore where the water was about three or four feet deep. Suddenly my feet could not find bottom. I slipped down the drop-off before I could call for help. With all of us splashing and talking I doubt if I would have been heard anyway. I bobbed to the top twice, flailing my arms, but I could not yell. I went down the third time, swallowing water. I recalled how the Lord had saved me from death when my appendix burst. Here I was again, facing what seemed inevitable death. But again God intervened. One of our neighbor's boys had heard me splash, and by chance or providence (I prefer the latter) swam my way. Suddenly my hand felt an arm. I clung to it and was pulled to shore by Rick Naaktgeboren. Quickly everyone was on shore surrounding me as I lay gasping on the ground. Fortunately I had not inhaled any water and I was soon on my feet. We felt guilty about our disobedience and were fearful lest we would never be permitted to swim again. We all made a pact of secrecy to tell no one, and it was years before my mother learned of my second escape from death.

Though the incident was soon only a memory for most of my friends, it proved to be much more than that for me. Why had I been saved? How did Rick know someone was drowning? By what coincidence did my hand find the arm of my friend under several feet of dark water? The answer was crystal clear: there was a purpose.

Life on the farm wasn't easy but it wasn't without its rewards. Harvest time meant working together with friends, neighbors, and relatives. We owe much to my Uncle Henk Plaggerman, who had married my mother's sister, Annie Mol. He showed us how to plant corn, when to cut hay, and a dozen other secrets of successful farming.

Stacking grain bundles became a cooperative task with the five Schut boys, Uncle Henk's two boys, and Uncle Henk working together. That he was able to tolerate all of our foolishness was an indication of the greatness of this man. Since I had had some experience in stacking grain, I was selected to do that job. Because pitching the bundles from the bundle rack to the stack took strength, Uncle Henk did all the pitching. The other boys went to the field to refill the second rack. Bert W. was older than I and sometimes helped with the stacking, but he had trouble keeping his balance on the round slippery bundles. I often thought he was very clumsy. Or could there be another reason for his unsteadiness? I didn't want to think about it.

Horses were the only source of power, and we constantly compared the horses owned by the three families. Uncle Henk had the largest horses, and they were easily the winners when it came to pulling power. But their comparative ability to run swiftly was a continuing source of discussion and disagreement. Aunt Artie owned a horse named Savage, and Uncle Henk owned a horse named Maude. Both horses were known to be swift. Cousin Jim Schut was always contending with Cousin Bert Plaggerman that their Savage could beat Maude in a race anywhere, anytime. Uncle Henk didn't say too much at first, but the constant boasting and counter-boasting finally got to him.

"Why don't we settle this once and for all and have a race?" he said.

We had lots of grain to stack and the race meant taking the harness off both horses and putting it back on again. But what did that matter when there was an argument to settle?

Jim mounted his horse, Savage, and Bert Plaggerman jumped on his horse, Maude. The race was across a quarter-mile field and back. The horses raced neck and neck most of the way, but shortly before the last lap Savage forged ahead. That was a triumph for Jim, but Uncle Henk wasn't satisfied.

So he challenged Jim by saying, "I bet Maude will win if I ride her."

"I bet she can't," replied Jim, so away they went again. This time the results were reversed, and Maude came in first. This was more fun than stacking grain, so we all started to wonder if any of the other horses were faster than Maude.

But Uncle Henk said, "I think we have had enough foolishness for one day."

So back to work. But the argument still wasn't settled. And it never was.

Although we were aware that our family disease would probably claim some of the cousins on my father's side, the subject was seldom discussed. After Pa's death there were no visible signs of the disease for several years, and with the hope and visions of youth we made no effort to try to find out the possibilities of becoming affected. We knew it was hereditary, but we knew little about the laws of genetics and how they applied to the disease in our family.

I had seen every phase of the disease as it slowly progressed in my father's body, and the symptoms were indelibly imprinted on my mind. Now I began to understand the "clumsiness" of my cousin Bert W. Each time I visited or worked with him I noticed the unmistakable early symptoms of the disease. He stumbled often. His laugh and cough seemed "different." His handwriting lacked the fluent, flowing curves it had once displayed.

Questions came to my mind. Did Bert W. realize he was clumsy? Did he know these were symptoms of the disease? Was he ready to admit the possibility of having only ten years to live. Should I talk to him about it? What would his reaction be? What would we do if I did confront him with the idea of doing something about it? But what hope could I offer? What hope could anyone offer him? Our fathers had spent hundreds of dollars in Rochester, only to discover that there was no cure. Bert W. was only twenty years old and had so much to live for. To do nothing meant inevitable death. Some doctor might know more about the disease now than was known fifteen years earlier. My decision was made. I would talk to Bert W. about the possibility of his having the disease, and ask if he would be willing to seek help. The long fight had begun.

6

The Fight Begins

Bert W. and I had much in common—we went to the same church and to many of the same parties. When we discussed our religious convictions we were in complete agreement. Still, I found it very difficult to approach him about his symptoms.

On one beautiful, summer evening, at a party given in honor of a friend's birthday, no one was in a hurry to go inside to play games. As I saw Bert W. standing with a group of boys, trying to keep his balance and laughing in that characteristic slurring manner, I knew that if ever I was to talk to him about it, I would have to do so soon.

I walked slowly up to him and said, "Let's go for a ride."

"OK," he replied.

We got into my car and drove off. We talked about the farm work and the need for rain.

"Bert," I suddenly blurted out, "I've noticed lately that you can't walk as well as you used to. Do you find it hard to keep your balance?"

He stared at me with eyes that expressed both fear and disbelief and said nothing.

We drove a little further and I stopped beside the road. I turned toward him and quietly said, "Bert, I don't know how to say this, but I've noticed that for the last year you haven't been able to work as well as when you were younger. Tell me, haven't you noticed it yourself?"

He looked away and with a quiver in his voice quietly replied, "Yeah, I have."

"Have you ever thought about seeing a doctor about it?" I asked.

"Yes, but what's the use? They can't do anything."

"How do you know if you don't try?"

"They couldn't do anything for our fathers, could they?"

"But that was many years ago, and a lot of new things have been discovered since then."

Silence.

"You know as well as I do what will happen if you don't do anything," I continued. "You have nothing to lose."

"Well, what do you suggest?" he asked.

"I would like to have you go to the University of Minnesota Hospital and have a thorough examination. Maybe the doctors there can give you some help."

"But how do I tell Mom?" he asked. "Maybe she doesn't know it yet."

"Don't you think she does? She lived with your father for years when he had it. She's probably afraid to talk to you about it, thinking that she might upset you."

"Somehow I can't get myself to talk to her about it. She has so many problems already, and we don't have any money to pay for doctor or hospital bills."

"Perhaps if we talk to Dr. Bendix about it he can get some help free. They may even do some research on it since it's such a strange disease."

"But I can't tell Mom," he insisted.

"Will you let me go with you? We'll talk to her together."

"I'm afraid she'll get terribly upset and I don't want to do that to her."

Then I began to get angry.

"Do you just want to do nothing and die? You know, Bert, I may be in the same situation as you are pretty soon. How about our eight brothers and sisters? I just can't sit idly by and do nothing. I just won't!"

There was a long pause.

"All right," he finally said. "Let's get going. Let's hope and pray that something can be done. If not for us, then for the next generation. I know one thing, I'm not going to get married and pass it on to my children."

A week or so later I drove to their farm. Bert W. and I found Aunt Artie alone, washing the dishes.

"Mom," Bert said, "We want to talk to you about something."

"Well, what is it now?" she asked, expecting some new crazy brainstorm of ours. Then she noticed our seriousness. She wiped her hands on her apron and sat down.

"Henry," Bert W. said, "you tell her."

I hesitated, but there was no way out.

"Aunt Artie," I started, "Bert and I have been talking about the trouble he has with walking. We are afraid he's getting the same disease Uncle Will had. And he and I think he should go to a doctor and have an examination."

"There's nothing wrong with Bert," Aunt Artie retorted. "He can work just as hard as you can."

I wasn't prepared for an answer like that, but Bert W. had anticipated his mother's reaction.

"Mom, you know it takes me so long to tie my shoes, and it's so hard for me to write."

He stopped a moment as Aunt Artie turned her eyes toward him.

"And look, Mom, I can't stand up with my eyes closed without losing my balance."

He stood up by his chair, closed his eyes and released his hold on the chair. He started to reel, then quickly opened his eyes and caught himself on a nearby table.

48

Aunt Artie jumped up from her chair, threw her arms around him, and started to cry.

"Oh, Bert," she cried, "I've been so afraid that you or Alice would get it!"

Then the words came tumbling out.

"I just can't believe that you will have to go through the same thing your Pa went through. I've been watching Alice and thought that since she's older she would show it first, and I'm so afraid. She isn't walking very well either."

She stopped momentarily and bowed her head. "Oh, God, what do we do now? Help us to know Your will."

"Let's ask Dr. Bendix if he has any ideas," I suggested. After more discussion, Aunt Artie agreed.

Within a few days we went to see Dr. Bendix, our doctor in Annandale, who in turn made arrangements to have Bert W. admitted to the University Hospital in Minneapolis.

He spent the greater part of a week there and was given extensive tests. Among them was a spinal tap to determine if there were any abnormalities in the chemical composition of the spinal fluid.

Two doctors at the hospital took a special interest in the disease and diagnosed it as a possible degeneration of a part of the cerebellum, the rear and bottom part of the brain. They told us that this part of the brain controlled the smooth functioning of most of the muscle actions we perform without consciously thinking about them. Walking, talking, writing, and many other actions, they said, are done almost automatically. Once the mind makes a decision to walk, the process of placing one foot in front of the other and keeping one's balance is taken over by the cerebellum.

Now they were ready to give a name to our family disease. The characteristic symptoms — a staggering walk, slurring speech, and the inability to perform more intricate motions—are common, they said, to a disease called "ataxia." The existence of a disease of this nature had first been

49

discovered in 1863 by the German scientist N. Friedreich. A particular strain of ataxia was further identified as "hereditary cerebellar ataxia" in 1893 by the Frenchman Pierre Marie. Our family disease, said the doctors, was of this type, often called "Marie's Ataxia."

The fact that our fathers' family had been so severely affected was of special interest to these doctors, and they asked us to make a family tree. This we immediately agreed to do.

But the big and important question remained: "Can you find a cure?"

"We'll try."

They could promise no more than that.

These two doctors came out from the university to our home and to Aunt Artie's home. I spent a great deal of time with them as they gave many of our relatives neurological examinations. Needless to say, we were happy that at long last someone was taking an active interest in our family problem. Hopes were raised that perhaps there was a cure. But the experience was not a completely happy one, because they confirmed our fears that Alice was also showing the first symptoms. Now we had one more reason to try to find a cure. If a cure was not found, it meant only ten years to live for two people whom we all loved.

The doctors told us that when we had completed our family tree and had indicated on it who had been affected, they would be able to determine the genetic pattern of the disease. Then they would be able to predict more accurately the probability of its progress in our generation.

The task of preparing a family tree fell on me. I started by asking Mom all she knew about Pa's family. Then I wrote Aunt Nell, my father's sister, who had not been affected by the disease. She had been only six years old when her mother died of the disease. Her mother's maiden name was Vanden Berg, she said, and there were others in the

Vanden Berg family who had had the disease. Her grand-father, Gerrit Jan Vanden Berg, had died of it, but as far as she knew, not any of my grandfather Schut's family had been affected. This information sent me looking up the Vanden Berg family tree instead of the Schut family tree.

Aunt Nell told me about an old man who was a distant cousin, and suggested that I talk to him. He had emigrated from the Netherlands and had known many members of the Schut and Vanden Berg families—many of whom had re-mained in the Netherlands.

Lambert Vanden Berg lived in Sioux Center, Iowa. He was eighty-two years old when I went to visit him. He had a keen, alert mind and was able to fill in many of the details of the family and the disease. His father (a brother of my great-grandfather Vanden Berg) had not been affected by the disease, and neither had any of his father's descendants. Several of his father's brothers and sisters had contracted the disease, however, and in every case they had passed it on to a number of their descendants.

The doctors had told us that if the disease had a "dominant hereditary pattern," only those who had the disease could pass it on to their descendants. Lambert's information verified this fact.

With the help of the doctors in the university I was able to build the family tree as it is found in this book. We knew it would need to be brought up to date as new facts were discovered, but the older generations were accurately set up at that time.

Alice, now about twenty-five, was not convinced that she had the disease. Aunt Artie always defended her if any of us indicated that she wasn't able to perform some of the more intricate movements as well as she used to. Even when her piano playing began to deteriorate, Aunt Artie per-sistently found some other explanation. With characteristic optimism, Alice seemed to enjoy life. She had become more slender as she grew older, and we had to find new ways to tease her. She was a good cook and loved to bake cakes and cookies. With seven boys who loved to eat, she had a difficult time keeping her creations from being devoured before they were cool. She finally resorted to hiding the goodies as they were baked, but our keen noses usually led us to the hiding place. Aunt Artie and Alice often became very angry with us, and understandably so. In spite of all this Alice was a very loving person and always gave us an affectionate hug whenever we came over for a visit.

Sometime later the doctors visited us again. We called the members of the family together.

"What is the possibility of a cure being found?" I asked.

"The causes for these hereditary neurological diseases are very baffling and we can only come up with theories. Since a cure is usually a result of finding a cause, we just can't promise that we can find a cure, or if there ever will be one," replied Dr. Gray.

Bert W. looked at him with pleading eyes. "Do you mean to tell me that there isn't even the *hope* of a cure?"

"That is right. I can't offer you or your sister any hope at the present time. If there is a cure it will take years of research to find it, long after it would help you or Alice."

"Then we must just continue to get worse and worse until we die?"

"I don't want to be brutal, and I truly sympathize with you, but I don't feel I should offer you a false hope."

"What about us who don't have it yet?" I asked. "Isn't there something we could do to prevent it, or at least know if we will become afflicted?"

"Really not. We can diagnose the disease definitely when we see certain symptoms. I'm quite sure that if you are honest with yourself you will be aware of some of the symptoms before anyone else. But don't interpret just any stumble or fall as a symptom. Remember, everybody falls at times.

I don't know if this is much consolation, but keep in mind that you also have a fifty-fifty probability of *not* becoming a victim."

"But isn't there anything we can do?" asked Bert W.

"Not for yourself—but you can do something for the future. You can decide never to have children."

"But I won't make that decision," declared Henk emphatically. "No one has a right to ask me to do that!"

Dr. Gray swung around in his chair and faced Henk. "That may be true," he replied, "but you must consider what it means to bring more people into the world who must face a future like your brother Bert. Do you have a right to do that?"

"I'm not sure that I'm willing to make that decision either," I added. "At least, not until I know for sure that I have it. After all, I still have that fifty-fifty chance of not getting it.

"Listen, Henry, in your family all you need to do is wait until you are thirty years old. If you don't show any symptoms you can still raise a family. That doesn't seem such a sacrifice to me when you consider the alternative. It's the only medicine I have to offer."

In principle I agreed. But for me the medicine was too bitter, and I couldn't swallow it at that time.

We had had such high hopes that we could find some help, but now we were a dejected group.

"Don't worry," said Mom. "God will show us a way."

But we couldn't share her optimism and faith.

7

The Hurts of Social Stigma

The event of going to the hospital and the visits of the two doctors to our homes had not gone unnoticed by the community. The disease had been officially diagnosed as "Marie's Hereditary Cerebellar Ataxia" by the doctors, but in the local community it soon became known as "Schut's disease"—a term we came to despise.

We now had two battles to fight. One fight was against the disease itself, and the other was the struggle against the social stigma that came with it. We found the battle against the social stigma to be as heartbreaking and difficult as the battle against ataxia.

Our young people's group was very closely knit. Many of us were related to each other, and nearly all of us were of Dutch descent. Our social lives were mostly confined to our church friends and neighbors. We loved and cared for each other. There were the usual hurts, heartaches, and occasional fights that all teenage groups have, but we enjoyed being together. Most of us lived on farms and had to work hard, but our work made us physically strong and healthy.

We Schuts were often the life of the party. My brother, Bert J., was especially popular; his wit and humor could make any party a gala affair. His popularity with the girls made him the envy—and sometimes the enemy—of other boys.

My own attraction for and from the opposite sex was much more limited—limited, in fact, to one young lady. Hazel and I had gone to the same church and catechism classes for years, but I hardly knew she existed until she was fifteen years old and I was seventeen. Suddenly she became a very attractive young lady. To my chagrin, a number of other boys made the same discovery about the same time. Hazel's mother had died when she was two years old, and she had since made her home with her paternal grandparents. She was about medium build, with blue eyes and brown hair. Somewhat bashful and timid, she blushed easily, which was in keeping with her fine character.

During the summer we had two church services each Sunday. A Dutch service was held in the morning and an English service and Sunday school in the afternoon. During the winter months only one service was held during the day, with services on alternate Sundays in the Dutch language. Over the years the Dutch services diminished to only one each month.

Many of us young people questioned why there should be any Dutch services at all. Very few people attended who could not understand English, and we felt they didn't *want* to learn it. The Dutch services were long, the sermons frequently lasting an hour or more. I never got much out of them—not because I couldn't understand them, but primarily because I rebelled against the whole idea. The Dutch psalms that we sang at these services had beautiful tunes, but the tempo was too slow. The young people wanted to change to the faster-moving hymns. We sometimes stayed outside and discussed the events of the week instead of attending the Dutch service. We listened to the singing, and when the last psalm was being sung we quietly sneaked into the vestibule and mingled with the departing congregation. The deception was exposed one Sunday when our parents asked us what the sermon was about. We solved that problem by having one or two of us attend the service and quickly share with the others the high points of the sermon.

Our mother wasn't very gullible, however, and we seldom got away with it. She didn't make a big issue of it, but she did indicate her displeasure. She pointed out that neglecting one worship service would soon lead to the neglect of other Christian responsibilities, and soon we would find excuses for not attending church at all. We loved and respected her and knew she spoke to us out of concern for our good. She wanted us to be prepared to conquer the temptations that lay ahead.

C.E. (our name for the Christian Endeavor Society) was held in the evening and was a welcome change. One of the members was given the responsibility of leading the group on an assigned topic relevant to our spiritual life and growth. The leader chose different persons to participate by speaking on the topic or reading a short poem related to it. We sang lively gospel songs. A series of sentence prayers by those who wished to participate closed our meetings. The closing benediction, repeated in unison, was always "Now may the Lord watch me and thee while we are absent from one another."

Our pastor usually attended our C.E. meetings—partly to indicate an interest in young people and partly to assure that we maintained a proper reverence. This was sometimes necessary as there were some of us who did not have an hour-long interest span in religious matters. After the C.E. meeting was over, we spent thirty to sixty minutes talking, visiting, and deciding who was going home with whom. It was after one of these meetings that I got up the courage to walk up to Hazel. Trying to be matter-of-fact,

I said, "Come on, let me take you home." To my surprise, she accepted.

We arrived at her home, about a mile away, and sat in the car only a short time before she said, "I better go in the house or Grandpa Dalman may come after me."

I didn't think I was such a dangerous person to be with, but how do you disagree with a reason like that?

The next week I took her home again and then asked for a date. She could go with me, I suggested, to a new movie entitled "Wings," which was showing in nearby Maple Lake the next Friday evening. She hesitated a moment and replied, "I don't think Grandpa will let me go." She stopped a moment and continued, "Grandpa doesn't want you to take me home anymore. He thinks I'm too young."

I expressed my disappointment, but I couldn't blame Hazel. I wasn't brave enough to discuss the matter with Hazel's grandpa, and I also knew it wouldn't change the situation. So I went home a discouraged young man.

My brother Bert J. and cousin Henk had similar experiences with other girls. We did not consider it too much of a problem at first as there were plenty of girls we could date. But as we grew a few years older the pattern recurred over and over again. Bert W. became more disabled and his sister Alice began to show symptoms that everybody could diagnose. Soon we began to hear through various sources that the parents of the young people we dated were concerned about their sons and daughters falling in love with the Schuts. No one wanted their child to marry someone who might be an invalid in a few years and die before the age of forty.

The problem of acceptance often became the subject of our conversation when we visited each other. Was it fair for parents to forbid their sons and daughters to date us? We concluded that parents were justified if the disease was already present in the person, but that they were cruel in making a blanket judgment against all of us.

There were whispers that the disease might be contagious, and some parents even suggested that it might be best if their children did not come into our homes. These rumors were cruelest of all, but with the ignorance about hereditary diseases prevalent at the time, it was understandable.

One doctor had even indicated that our family might have syphilis, which sometimes causes locomotor ataxia, a disease with symptoms somewhat similar. Could it be true that our grandparents had been immoral people? Everybody we talked with said, "No, your parents and grandparents were all persons with high moral character and strong Christian principles." Yet, we reasoned that perhaps Grandpa or Grandma had not been as good as people claimed.

We had to know. Did we carry a germ that could be transmitted to someone else or passed on to our children? Three of us decided to contact the university hospital. We had heard that a test could determine if we carried the syphilis germ—a blood test and spinal test called the Wasserman test. The doctors who had previously examined my cousin Bert W. told us they had found nothing. Furthermore, they told us that syphilis had additional symptoms, none of which any of us exhibited. We still insisted that we wanted to have a Wasserman test. The doctors consented. There was no evidence of syphilis.

"In a certain sense you are unfortunate that your family does not have syphilis," they said. "We can treat that. But the ataxia in your family is a genetic trait and is incurable. There is only one way to eliminate it. That is not to reproduce."

The hopelessness of the situation resulted in profound differences among us. Some thought, "If I can't enjoy a long life, I'll get in as much enjoyment as I can while it lasts." Others chose to ignore it and live as normally as possible. Others became bitter against God for placing such a burden on a person. Others chose to accept the disease as something God used to bring out their faith and courage. A few were stoical; they merely shrugged their shoulders and said, "Whatever will be, will be." But nearly all of us decided that the less we talked about it the better, because there was no way we could communicate to others the hurt that we felt.

In my own mind there was a struggle. Would keeping quiet about the disease solve any problems? Yet I also knew that any explanation would not be understood. Nor did I know whether I could justify my feelings toward the parents who discouraged their sons and daughters from marrying us. Could I blame them if they wanted to prevent their child from becoming the wife or husband of someone who had a fifty-fifty chance of becoming an invalid? Could I expect parents to encourage a marriage if many of their grandchildren would get this dreaded disease? The answers to these questions were obvious. No parent would knowingly subject his son or daughter to that risk. Even Grandpa Mol had said, "If I had known that the Schut boys might get that disease I would certainly have tried to stop the marriages."

It was common knowledge, of course, that at least two of us had the symptoms. I also knew that people were watching my brother Bert J. and me, to see if we were walking steadily or talking clearly. People who meant well came to me and suggested that perhaps I should not work so hard. We kept checking our own actions. Bert J. and I often walked a one-inch board fence to prove to ourselves that we could keep our balance. We welcomed any opportunity to compare ourselves with others and spared no effort to prove that we could compete and even excel.

The fear of those first symptoms was our constant companion. There were times when I was certain that I was showing them, and as I watched Bert J. I often thought his walking wasn't quite normal. In the wintertime as I walked around in the snow doing the farm chores I took note of the tracks I had made earlier in the day. Was this step off to one side? Was it an attempt to catch my balance? Or had I slipped on the ice and jumped to one side to keep from falling, the reaction of any normal person?

Yet we couldn't make our life plans on the assumption that we would positively become afflicted. The doctors had told us that we had also a fifty-fifty chance of *not* having the disease. But to be well and to have brothers and sisters who were afflicted precluded any attempt for a completely normal life. Our lives were too closely intertwined to permit that.

8

Struggling for an Education

I was now twenty years old. I had always wanted to continue my education but couldn't because of the responsibilities at home. My brother Bert J. was now eighteen years old and capable of operating the farm. Now I felt I could start high school if I could drive to Annandale, which was about nine miles away. I could still help with the chores and farm work after school and on Saturdays.

One day I approached Mom with the idea. She said, "Why, what do you want to learn for?"

No one went to high school unless he had plans to become trained in some profession.

"Ever since the Lord healed me after being so sick I have wanted to become a doctor," I answered. "Perhaps I can find a cure for ataxia or become a medical missionary."

Mom was thrilled. "I'm glad you want to do that, but I don't know how we can manage to help you. There isn't any money."

"I'm sure the Lord will show the way," I replied.

Shortly after I made the decision to go to high school, providence provided the circumstances by which I could begin dating Hazel again. When she became seventeen she began working in different homes. This meant she was not under the strict supervision of her grandfather. I had dated other girls and she had dated other boys, but I really felt she was the girl I could love. She had all the qualities of a great person and she was a Christian, which meant a lot to me.

We dated for several months and found out that our feelings for each other were mutual. We soon were "going steady."

But I had made plans for the future that made marriage an impossibility for many years. Did I have a right to ask Hazel to wait for years while I completed my education? Did she realize that I still had a fifty-fifty chance of getting ataxia? She was a popular girl and could certainly find someone who would marry her soon and who had a better chance of a long life. Sometimes I even wondered whether I should continue my education. It was possible that by the time I completed it I would be disabled by ataxia. Why not forget it, get married, and enjoy as much of life as I had left? There seemed to be many reasons why I should not go on to school. Yet the desire to go was so great that I decided to go through with it, whatever the cost.

There were no school buses coming as far as our home, but there were several other young people living nearby who wanted to go to high school. I approached them about the possibility of riding together, and soon I had four others who would share the expenses of driving to Annandale.

We had to buy our own textbooks, either new or used. Since there were no provisions for lunches, we took them with us from home. Unless it was extremely cold we left them in the car and went there to eat. Often, by mutual agreement, we exchanged our lunches. Sometimes the sandwiches were a little frozen, but we thawed them, bite by bite, with swallows of hot cocoa from the thermos bottle.

We usually didn't have much trouble with our '27 Chevrolet but on several occasions the transmission locked in two forward gears, resulting in no movement at all. We always carried some tools with which we could unfasten the eight bolts that held down the shifting lever plate. We then pushed the gears in place with a screwdriver and replaced the plate. We learned a lot about cars during that time.

Although the opportunity to date Hazel was limited because of finances, we learned to love each other deeply. One beautiful June evening we borrowed a boat from a friend and went rowing in the moonlight. The weather was warm, and the dry weather had killed all the mosquitoes.

We beached the boat and sat under a tree on the shore. The moonlight reflected its light on the water, which rippled in glistening waves. Far across the lake a loon called for its mate and all was quiet. All the doubts about whether we should share our lives vanished.

It was there on the shore of beautiful Sugar Lake that we made a personal commitment to each other for life. We talked of our love for each other and the problems we might face.

"Are you willing to wait for me until I have finished school?" I asked. "It may take five or six years."

"I realize that. But I'm willing to wait."

"Do you realize that I may have only ten or fifteen years to live if I get ataxia?"

"Yes, I've thought a lot about that. Some of my relatives have talked to me about it. But I would rather live with you for ten years than have a long life with anyone else."

I had not dared to hope that I could be that fortunate. I knew the commitment we had made to each other would be kept.

During my last year of high school I felt it was too expensive to drive to school. The car was getting old, breakdowns were frequent, and the depression of 1933 was at its worst. I was able to find a place to stay about a mile from Annandale. There I earned my room and board by helping with the chores and working on Saturdays. I could ride into Annandale on a wagon bus in the summer and on a sleigh in the winter. There was no heat in the bus, but with fifteen to twenty students in it and being enclosed, it was better than walking. The bus was pulled by two horses, and our speed ranged from two to ten miles per hour. In the summer I often walked or ran to my boarding home and got home sooner.

In June, 1933, at the age of twenty-three, I graduated from high school at the top of my class. With the help of several interested teachers and a God-given ability to learn easily, I had been able to complete the four-year course in three years. We could not afford a junior-senior banquet or class rings, but we did get diplomas.

I then needed to earn money for college tuition. I obtained work with a farmer and received $17.50 per month for three months. I was able to receive a scholarship of $100 from Central College, in Pella, Iowa, one of the Christian colleges of the Reformed Church in America. I enrolled in the fall of 1933.

My first year I roomed with my cousins Jim and Harold who were already attending. Jim was one year ahead of me, even though he was six years younger. Harold, also younger, was three years ahead of me. Both had entered college as soon as they had completed high school. My summer's earnings of fifty-two dollars did not pay for much food or for a room. By buying day-old bread, getting eggs from some relatives in the country, and taking canned meat along from home we made meals of rice beef soup, milk, oatmeal, meat, and eggs. We survived quite well.

Thanksgiving time came quickly, and I had not seen Hazel or my family since September. How could we get home? We had no money. We did, however, have a classmate whose father bought fruit in Iowa and sold it in Albert Lea, Minnesota. Jim and I decided to ride 160 miles with him and try to hitchhike the rest of the way.

We started from Pella about nightfall the day before

Thanksgiving. It was totally dark in the back of the truck where we and the apples were, but warm enough to be comfortable with our heavy coats. We had driven an hour when our driver stopped. He opened the door and asked, "How would you like some company?"

We said, "Sure, there's lots of room back here."

We thought he had stopped to pick up some friends who wanted to go to Albert Lea, but to our surprise two women hitchhikers climbed into the rear of the truck. We had no idea what they looked like, how old they were, or who they were. Jim and I tried to start a conversation but they were very quiet and perhaps afraid. We never did find out who they were or where they were going. Intermittently we slept while we sat on the baskets of apples. About daylight we arrived at a gas station near Albert Lea, and our unknown companions left to catch another ride. We arrived at the home of our classmate early in the morning and were treated to a good hot breakfast. The driver asked us how we got along with the girls.

"They didn't bother us at all," we said.

I don't know whether he believed us or not, but I saw a smirk on his face. We were sure he stopped to pick up these girls just to embarrass us.

At 8 A.M. we were still 150 miles from home. We had stood by the road only a short time when a truck with a flat bed stopped. The driver asked, "Do you want to ride on the back of the truck?"

"How far are you going?"

"To Minneapolis," he answered.

That is where we wanted to go, but riding in the open with the temperature around 25 degrees wasn't a pleasant prospect. We decided we could always try for another ride when he stopped. But he never stopped. When we got to the south side of Minneapolis we were so cold and stiff we could hardly walk.

We then took a streetcar to a road intersection on the north side of Minneapolis. Two rides later I stepped out at our driveway and surprised the family by walking in the door. They did not know I was coming home. The trip cost us thirteen cents, the streetcar fare across Minneapolis.

My first thought was how to get to see Hazel. It was nearly evening and brother Bert said, "There's a party tonight and I'm sure Hazel will be there." Bert J. and I drove out to the party and I had someone tell Hazel that someone wanted to see her outside. We were very happy to be reunited after three months of separation.

Getting back to college for the three weeks between Thanksgiving and Christmas posed quite a problem. After some planning between our family and Jim's family we decided to take our old '27 Chevrolet back to college. It took the combined sacrifice of both families to provide the funds for the gas, but the plan provided a means of getting home again for the Christmas holidays. We did make the trip to Iowa, but one of the connecting rods in the motor was nearly burned out so we had to replace that between Thanksgiving and Christmas.

The trip back to Minnesota took over twenty-four hours because of the snow and a car breakdown. We were able to return to college with a cousin, Joe Ernissee, who had a car and also attended Central College.

I discovered that college competition was stiff and that I could not match the ability of some of my classmates, but I did well nevertheless. I took a premed course and loved it, but now found myself to be completely penniless. My mother and brother were as financially destitute as I was. I was discouraged and somewhat bitter. Why did God give me the ability to learn and then not provide the means? Why did ataxia have to rob our family of its main provider? At the end of the first semester I told my advisor I had no choice but to quit.

But help was on the way. The country was in the midst of the 1933 depression. Unemployment was high and wages very low. A new government administration took over and initiated a program called Students Relief Employment (S.R.E.). Jim and I applied and were accepted. We were given jobs such as cleaning bricks, dismantling old buildings, cleaning dormitories, and painting farmhouses that were owned by the college. This helped pay for our tuition and books. But we still had to find something to eat.

My chemistry professor offered to provide us with one-half gallon of milk per day on credit. It seemed that the college owned several farms, but the farmers could not pay their rent. So the farmers agreed to pay their rent in milk, meat, and eggs. The college in turn paid the professors part of their salaries in produce. With the help of a few dollars from Hazel and from home we managed to survive.

After getting back to college after Christmas vacation there seemed to be no way I could get back home until June. Hazel and I were getting very lonesome for each other, so I suggested that perhaps she could find housework in Pella. She came by bus in early February and found work on a farm about five miles out in the country. It paid two dollars per week. I had no way to get out there except by occasionally borrowing my cousin's Model T Ford. I would put in one gallon of gas, fifteen cents worth (which Hazel paid for), and we could spend some time together on the farm. We wished we could see each other more often, but it was better than being 330 miles apart.

As spring arrived the weather became very dry and hot. Soon the dust storms of 1934 began creating havoc with the crops. There were days when sun was invisible. Back home in Minnesota the drought was even worse. The crops had been planted, but there was no moisture for seed to grow. There was no grass for the cattle, nor was there hay for the winter ahead.

My brother, Bert J., had been operating the farm with the help of my younger brothers John (fourteen) and Bill (twelve). It was a very discouraging situation. He wrote that he had an opportunity to ride to California and would like to work there during the summer. He had to leave before I could get home so my cousin Henry W. did the chores for a week.

Before leaving for home I had to repay the college the money I had borrowed. I agreed to do so by painting a house the college owned. It was my good fortune that the house I had to paint was the one in which Hazel was working. We spent four wonderful days together.

But our happy days sped by all too rapidly, and the time came for me to leave. Hazel couldn't go with me because the woman she was working for was too ill to care for her family. So early on May 31, 1934, I began my trip home, hitchhiking. It proved to be the hottest day on record. In Mason City, Iowa, I walked up to a home and asked for a drink, which the folks graciously gave me. Their thermometer registered 111 degrees in the shade at 11 A.M. I was given several rides which left me stranded out in the country without shade. I was nearly overcome by the heat when a couple going to Minneapolis picked me up. Thank God for that couple, who not only gave me a ride to Minneapolis, but bought me a good meal and wished me Godspeed.

It was dark when I arrived in Minneapolis, and since there was not much hope of hitchhiking home during the night, I took inventory of the funds I had left. I found I had enough to take a bus to a town about thirteen miles from home; from there I could make a phone call to my mother.

It was 11 P.M. before I arrived home—a hot and weary but very happy young man.

I was now twenty-four years old and had completed my high school education and one year of college. At the time

The author with his parents, John and Jennie Schut, in front of the old farm home, 1911.

The author's father, John Schut, as a young man.

The author's mother, Jennie Mol Schut, at age 62, 1945.

Artie Mol Schut, 1960.

The male Schut-Mol cousins, about 1930 (l. to r.): Bill, John, Wilbert, James, Harold, Henry W., Henry J., Bert W., and Bert J.

The home place, 1957.

The author (right) on the farm with his son Lawrence and brother William, 1938.

The Reformed Church of Silver Creek, Minnesota, 1961.

Dr. John Schut, 1947.

Dr. John Schut, 1954.

Bert J. Schut with Dr. John Schut and John's wife, Mary, shortly before John's death, 1971.

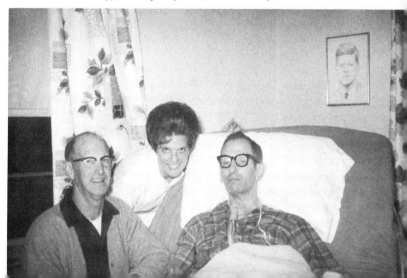

Henry J. and Hazel Schut.

I was confident that I would be able to return to college in September. I didn't know how or where the money was to come from, but surely God would provide a way.

But my immediate task was to assume the job of operating the farm, since my brother Bert J. had left a week before. It was a nearly hopeless task. There was no pasture, no feed for the cattle, and no prospect for rain. The roadsides had some dry grass, so we herded the cattle along the roadside ditches for a time and we fenced in the grain fields for pasture. About a week after I arrived home a heavy rain came. Even though it was late in the season I immediately planted some corn and some millet seed for hay. The corn grew rapidly and produced some feed, but the grain crop produced one load of bundles—just enough for seed for the next year.

The problems on the farm were further complicated by extremely low prices. Live hogs sold for two dollars a hundredweight, butterfat for sixteen cents a pound, and eggs for seven cents a dozen. There was no way we could pay the bills, and there were times we didn't have three cents for a postage stamp.

Fortunately the government was sympathetic. It refinanced the mortgage against our farm and also loaned us funds to buy feed which had to be shipped in from as far away as Oklahoma. We had to work on public works projects to repay the loans. And because the farm did produce enough food for us to eat, we were better off than many city workers who were standing in soup lines.

Ataxia was still very much a part of our life as Bert W. and Alice were slowly becoming more disabled. But for the time being the financial distress took priority over the problem of disease.

9

Seeking to Know God's Will

The summer passed swiftly, and I had to make plans to return to college. But those plans were contingent upon my brother Bert's return from California to operate the farm. Brother John was fourteen and brother Bill twelve, and both were in school. The school buses were now coming out from Annandale so John could go to high school.

Hazel returned from Iowa and found work in Minneapolis, receiving five dollars a week working in a home. We couldn't see each other very often as the cost of transportation was nearly equal to three days' wages. Nor could I go to Minneapolis for more than a half day since the milking had to be done. The decision to return to college was more difficult because of the problems it would make in our relationship.

To get married and go to college too was out of the question. Yet to be separated for prolonged periods of time was something neither of us was willing to accept.

I thought there might be one possible avenue open. I made an appointment with the Dean of the School of Medicine at the University of Minnesota.

The Dean asked me about my grades, my goals, my family, and finances. He spoke kindly and sympathetically. "Young man, you have the mental ability and the sincere desire to become a good doctor. But with your financial situation, your family responsibilities, and your age, you are trying to reach an impossible goal."

I tried to fight back my tears.

"I'm truly sorry to have to say that," he said, "but I've seen too many young men like you try to accomplish what you want to do, only to crack up emotionally and sometimes even commit suicide. They could not earn the money they needed to pay for their education, while at the same time keeping up the grades necessary for entering medical school. My sincere advice to you is to face the hard facts and decide that you will have to accept a vocation other than medicine."

"But I started high school at twenty with that goal in mind," I answered. "Aren't there scholarships or loans for people like me?"

"I'm afraid not," he replied. "The economy is so tight that many people don't even have enough to eat. That is the government's first responsibility."

I knew he was right. But a flurry of questions crowded my mind. Must I now go back home and admit that I had made a mistake? Must Hazel and I give up our dream of serving God in the medical field? Wasn't there somewhere a source from which money could be gotten? Wasn't there some way my mother and younger brothers could get along without my help? Was it my responsibility to be both father and brother to my younger brothers? Why did Pa and Mom have two more children when they knew he would not live to take care of them? I was not only broken-hearted but bitter. I went home that evening with a heavy heart.

That evening we visited Aunt Artie, and I watched Bert W. as he tried to walk—he could no longer run at all. He and Alice, I was reminded, had nothing to look forward to but disability and dying by inches, never knowing the love of a husband or wife or children. I had so much to

71

be thankful for. I had health and a wonderful girl who had promised to be my wife. There could be no room for self-pity.

God was soon to make. the decision for me regarding college. My brother Bert wrote that he definitely felt he should not come back to Minnesota. He didn't feel he could take the hurts of being stigmatized by the disease. Besides, God had found a good job for him. He was going to stay in California, and I could not blame him.

Hazel and I now had to rethink our whole future. Should we get married and finally give up any thought of my getting an education? Hazel was twenty-two and had not had a home of her own for seven years. We were both anxious to get married. But even if I didn't go to school, where would we live? I couldn't leave Mom and the family to shift for themselves. My sister Elsie was nineteen, working out, and earning some money—but only enough to support herself.

After agonizing over the different possibilities, Hazel and I decided that she should continue to work in Minneapolis while I stayed home and worked the farm. Perhaps a way might still be found for me to go back to college a year later.

We saw each other when we could, but seldom more than once or twice a month. We learned that our love could remain strong and grow, even if we could not be with each other very often. One thing that haunted us both was the possibility of my still getting ataxia. If I should get it, we would miss even the few years of normal life we could have together. Although I never doubted her love for me or her sincere desire to become my wife, I wondered if she still would want to share my life if I began showing signs of the disease. And would I have the right to expect her to do so? Why not forget the dream? Wasn't it obvious that God didn't want me to continue my education? Hadn't He indicated to me that my place was here at home in Silver Creek?

But I wasn't willing to accept that verdict—at least not yet.

That winter was a difficult one for all farmers. The price of feed was extremely high and that of farm produce very low. Many farmers were losing their farms or barely able to scrape together the payments to keep their property. Later that year, many were able to keep food on their tables only by working for the WPA (Work Projects Administration) building roads, planting trees, and making parks. They received thirty cents an hour—a big wage for that time.

In the spring, the drought broke and we had enough moisture for the seed to germinate. The alfalfa grew well enough to provide hay for the stock. The two D's, Drought and Depression, had brought us to the realization that we had to depend on God for everything.

I prayed daily that the Lord would keep me free from ataxia—not only for my sake but also for the sake of those I loved. It seemed that my prayers were being answered, but I could not be sure. My father had not shown any symptoms until he was in his middle thirties. I had at least ten years, then, before I could be certain, but the odds of my getting ataxia lessened each year.

As the summer progressed Hazel and I were forced into making a decision. We were both a year older, but the financial situation had not changed. My brothers, John and Bill, were still too young to operate the farm. Even if they would be able to do so in a year or two, it would mean they could not go on to high school.

I always marveled at my mother; she never seemed to be overly concerned. She did a considerable amount of worrying about our safety and moral behavior, but the financial problems she left to the Lord, or to me.

Hazel and I now made the inevitable decision—we would get married and abandon the impossible dream of college. It was a decision that brought very mixed emotions. We were happy that we would soon be husband and wife but disappointed that my plans for becoming a doctor would never be realized.

Having decided to marry, we made plans to live in an apartment we could make out of a couple of rooms upstairs in my mother's house. Mom and the boys would live downstairs, and I would operate the farm on a share-rent basis.

Our wedding took place on September 4, 1935. My brother Bert came from California to be my best man, and Hazel's sister, Sylvia, was the bridesmaid. We had a simple but beautiful wedding, paid for by Hazel's aunt and uncle, and we moved into our apartment the day after the wedding. There was no money for a honeymoon. I had to help fill silo the day after we moved into our home. We were very happy and accepted the change in our life plans as God's will. We decided to make our home a happy one.

We both loved children and wanted some of our own, but we wanted to wait until nearly all risk of getting ataxia was over. The idea of family planning was relatively new and not too acceptable in the social circles in which we lived, but under the circumstances we felt it was necessary. We considered sterilization, but decided that it was more permanent than what we wanted. If I was still free of the disease by the time I was thirty-one, we wanted to be able to start a family. We sought advice on family planning and read a book on it, but something went wrong. Our first son was born on September 13, 1936.

Lawrence James, the first grandchild of my mother and of Hazel's father, was immediately a celebrity. Our lives were full and very busy, but ataxia was never very far from our thoughts.

My cousin Bert W. went for a time to a distant cousin in Wisconsin to work on a farm. Soon the disease progressed so far that he was not able to earn his wages, so he returned home to Aunt Artie. He was a determined man and continued to help on the farm at home. Winter was a difficult time for him. The snow and ice caused him to fall frequently, and usually some part of his body was black and blue because of his tumbles. He devised a pair of ice shoes by driving short nails through short boards, then attaching them to his shoes with leather straps. The idea was helpful, but the weight of the ice shoes made it more difficult to walk and he soon had to discard them. There were times that he crawled to the barn on his hands and knees. Yet the burden never stifled his ever-ready smile; and to complain about his lot did not seem to occur to him.

The winter of 1938-39 brought colds and pneumonia to many people, and Bert W. had several severe sieges of illness. Each cold made him weaker and less able to ward off pneumonia. I spent many hours sitting by his bedside, trying to help him as he tried to cough up the phlegm that collected in his throat. Aunt Artie stayed with him most of the time, although others relieved her at times so she could get some rest. My mother spent hours helping with the household. At no time did I feel more helpless than when I sat by Bert W. as he coughed and nearly choked, then finally was able to bring up the phlegm and spit it out. He would then gasp for breath for several minutes and be relieved for a short time, only to go through the whole process again fifteen minutes later. There were times when his face became blue because his lungs were not able to receive the oxygen needed.

I recalled the time when we first discussed the possibility that he might have ataxia. It was now nearly ten years later. Although we had made some attempts to find help, very little had been accomplished. Alice was still quite well as the disease seemed to progress more slowly, but we knew that for her too there was only one possible conclusion.

Would I also have to go through this? Would my wife have to watch me die like this? And now we had a son and were expecting another child soon. Would they also have to face this prospect? I had been accused of taking the easy way because I had not made certain that we would not have children. Perhaps they were right.

10

To Die Is Gain

Hazel and I were eating supper and our son Lawrence was in his chair, awkwardly trying to cut his meat with a knife and fork.

Suddenly the telephone rang the familiar long and short ring which had been our family's ring on the party line for thirty years. We looked at each other and knew who was calling.

"We called Dr. Bendix this afternoon and he came out and examined Bert," blurted out Aunt Artie. "He told us Bert has pneumonia. Can you and your mother come over?"

"Yes," I answered. "As soon as I have the chores done."

When we arrived at Aunt Artie's home we saw some of the neighbors' cars on the yard and knew that Bert W. must be seriously ill. As we walked through the door we sensed the atmosphere that had been present at my father's death sixteen years earlier. Aunt Artie was crying. She walked up to Mom and they flung their arms around each other, neither one saying anything.

In the bedroom Bert W. recognized me and smiled weakly. He tried to say something but couldn't. I held his hand and told him I understood.

Bert W. had been coughing earlier in the day but now was no longer able to do so. His diaphragm had become paralyzed by ataxia, and there was no way he could expel the mucus from his lungs. His breathing became more rapid and shallow as more and more of his lungs became useless.

Aunt Artie walked back and forth from the kitchen to the bedroom, not knowing what to do. When she noticed that her presence seemed to excite Bert W. she remained in the kitchen. About an hour after we came he slipped into semiconsciousness, and his breathing stopped at times. I recognized the symptoms that had accompanied my father's death. As we and several of the neighbors stood quietly talking around the bed, Bert W. opened his eyes, looked at us, and smiled broadly. His breathing stopped, and life faded from his eyes. He died just three days before his thirtieth birthday.

A part of me died with Bert W. that evening. But the determination to do something to stop this disease became stronger than ever.

One of the suggestions that the doctors from the university had made was that they examine the brain of someone who had died of ataxia. An autopsy, they said, would be extremely helpful in determining what part of the brain was damaged.

There were several people present at Bert W.'s death who knew of the doctors' desire, and we discussed the matter among ourselves. Some felt Aunt Artie had been hurt too much already. Why should she be asked to submit a part of the body of her loved one to cold-hearted research? Yet we saw Alice standing right there, who in a matter of only a few years would be a victim of the same disease. In addition, there were eight others in our two families who could become affected. Didn't we owe them this chance of help?

Finally we decided to talk to Aunt Artie about it. It was an agonizing decision for her. It seemed sacrilegious to dismember a body of a loved one. Yet she knew that if something could be learned by studying the diseased brain, it could help her other four children. After some reluctance she gave her consent, and the necessary instructions were given to the mortician and the doctor.

The winter had been very cold and the grave had to be dug by hand with pick axes. Aunt Artie had no money to hire anyone to do the task, so some of the neighbors and I volunteered to provide a final resting place for the body of one of the first members of my generation to die of the disease.

Who would be next? How many more would come to this place prematurely? We didn't want to think about it.

The funeral took place on Bert W.'s thirtieth birthday. My grandfather Mol, now eighty years old, was dying of cancer but still able to attend the funeral. As the body was being viewed, he stood for quite some time and then quietly said, "Yes, Bert, you are in heaven, but I shall soon join you." Three months later they were united where there is no pain or disease.

The Rev. A. A. Dykstra was our pastor at the time, and he spoke very appropriately on the text, "For me to live is Christ, and to die is gain" (Philippians 1:21). For Bert W. it certainly was true. His body had no longer been able to respond to his will. Frustration had been his companion day and night. He had been a constant concern and care for his family. We could only echo our pastor's words.

But there was one person who could not accept that verdict so readily: my brother John. He was now nineteen and had entered college a year before. To him, Bert W.'s death at thirty years of age was not God's will, nor was death ever to be desired over life.

John's blue eyes could twinkle kindly when so disposed, but when his quick temper was aroused they seemed to shoot fire at the victim of his anger. He had a brilliant mind. In high school he quickly completed his assignments and then made life miserable for the teachers. Consequently he made frequent trips to the principal, who finally put him in a room by himself and gave him extra assignments. He was a hard and willing worker for someone else, but at home he often made life difficult for us. So he spent most of his high school years working for his room and board at a neighbor's farm.

Many times he had talked about going into medicine. I had encouraged him in this, feeling that he alone would have both the motivation and the intelligence to find a cure for ataxia.

"Motivation" turned out to be an understatement. John now undertook his premedical studies with a passion that completely possessed his life.

His race would be a race against time, since within ten years or less he might possibly display the same symptoms.

I was now twenty-nine and still well. A second son, Wayne, was born on June 25, 1939, a few months after Bert W. died. Hazel and I had so much to be thankful for. My brother Bert came home frequently and was still well. He had married in 1937 and was able to work hard.

The report on Bert W.'s autopsy showed that parts of his cerebellum had degenerated. We were told that this part of the brain coordinated and controlled all the messages from the brain to various parts of the body. The disease, as it were, had cut off the telephone lines between the central station and the muscles. Functions like walking, talking, coughing, laughing, and writing were affected. The ability to move the muscles smoothly and accurately gradually diminished, and when a vital muscle became affected, death was inevitable. But what caused it to happen? The doctors could not tell.

11

The Fight Intensifies

Life had to go on. Bert W. had been released from his nearly useless body. Now, more than ever, the concern for other possible victims was on the minds of all of us. We who were still in the risk age lived in dread fear that any day the first symptoms might appear. This was a frightening and indecisive process, because it was impossible to determine if some of the early symptoms, like stumbling and dropping objects, were just normal clumsiness or the first symptoms of ataxia.

As more and more of our cousins became twenty and older, many began to show the first symptoms. Letters began coming from other parts of the country, telling us that several of my cousins definitely had the disease and several others were suspected of showing the first signs. We also learned that some of the older cousins in Michigan, whom I had never known, had died of ataxia. There were or had been nineteen first cousins older than I and eighteen younger ones, besides many other distant cousins, who were "at risk," as we called those who had a chance of becoming afflicted.

I had begun to succeed in farming. World War II had begun in Europe and farm produce prices were rising. Cousin Harold had become a minister. Cousin Jim was in seminary. Another cousin, son of Aunt Grace, was also a pastor. They were all younger than I and were still "at risk" when Bert W. died.

After the University of Minnesota had examined Bert W.'s brain, they took renewed interest in the disease and sought patients they could study. When the news spread that research was being done, many of the cousins who were afflicted and those who were "at risk" came to visit us to see if they could help or get help.

In spite of the obvious fact that ataxia would not just "go away," some families refused to discuss it or seek help until they actually had the symptoms. This made it difficult for the doctors to get a complete picture of the disease in its various stages. It was as important to examine those who did not have ataxia as to examine those who did.

Many cousins left their home communities to start new lives in different states because of the stigma attached to the disease. If they became victims they frequently returned to their home communities. Here the rest of the family was able to give them the support and acceptance they needed.

Several years before, Ed De Kraai, a son of Aunt Carrie, had returned from Florida with the disease. (He was the young man who had scolded my father when he had gone on his cow-shooting spree.) Ed was about seven years older than I and had two younger sisters who were also "at risk" but were showing no symptoms as yet.

Ed was tall, dark, and handsome and possessed a pleasant smile, a good personality, and a proud spirit. He had been married while in Florida and had separated from his wife because his pride would not permit him to be dependent on her. He was still able to walk reasonably well and work at jobs that did not require a great amount of dexterity. He had difficulty in accepting his disability and tried hard to compensate for it by dressing neatly and being very polite when meeting other people.

Soon after he arrived at our home I made arrangements to have him enter the University of Minnesota Hospital for examination and research. He proved to be an excellent patient for research purposes as he was very cooperative and willing to stay in the hospital as long as necessary. He was the object of much study and many tests, but the results were always the same. The doctors knew what parts of the brain and body were affected, but they did not know why.

Ed was released from the hospital and worked in various places for several years. He was called to the University Hospital periodically so the doctors could note the progress of the disease. On one of these visits he encountered Dr. Rossen, a brilliant young neurologist who became deeply interested in helping Ed and studying the disease. In order to experiment on him with different drugs, Dr. Rossen made arrangements to have Ed become a permanent patient in the state hospital.

I visited Ed many times in St. Peter Hospital and always had the opportunity to sit down with Dr. Rossen and discuss Ed's condition and the condition of the other cousins who had the disease. On one of these occasions Dr. Rossen suggested that I organize a group of cousins who were willing to come down to St. Peter for several tests he had developed. This group was to include both those who were young enough to be "at risk" and those who were past the normal age of onset, the latter to be used as "controls."

The hospital was about a two-hour drive from our home, and some of us had to make arrangements for someone to do our chores. Before we set out we met at my home and had a prayer time, asking that God would bless our venture and that a clue toward a cure might be found.

On the way we stopped for a picnic dinner and temporarily forgot the seriousness of our journey. We were by nature a fun-loving group, and jokes, tricks, and stories made even a serious venture a jolly affair.

When we arrived at St. Peter State Hospital we had the opportunity to visit our cousin Ed, who had been a patient there for several years and was no longer able to walk. Ed had lost much of his fight to live, but still carried in his heart a pride that caused rifts in his relationship with his father. He could not, or would not, make the effort to bring about a reconciliation.

Dr. Rossen wanted to take samples of our spinal fluid and test it for a substance that he had found in an excessive amount in Ed's spinal fluid. I had had this done before in the University Hospital, and the doctors had not found any abnormality at that time. The spinal test was performed by inserting a long hollow needle between the vertebrae and suctioning out several cubic centimeters of the fluid. The process was painful or unpleasant and was sometimes followed by an intense headache. One of my cousins fainted after the test. The blood and urine tests were less of a problem, but the whole examination was unpleasant.

The neurological examination consisted of several simple tests. In one of these we were asked to walk on a straight line drawn on the floor. In another we stood up with our eyes closed to determine if we could keep our balance. We were also asked to stretch out our arms, close our eyes, and touch the end of our noses with our index fingers. Those with ataxia had difficulty performing these tests.

Except for those who already knew they had ataxia, the doctors found no symptoms. The blood, urine, and spinal tests would have to be studied, they said, and we would be notified. It gave us a measure of relief to know that some of us seemed to be free of the disease at that time.

Several weeks later a couple of us returned to St. Peter to discuss the chemical tests with Dr. Rossen and several other doctors. There seemed to be a higher than normal amount of one chemical in the spinal fluid of the victims, they said, but they were not certain of its significance. Dr. Rossen theorized that some chemical in the blood necessary to nourish the nerve cells was lacking, and that the excess chemical in the spinal fluid was a by-product of the degeneration of the nerve cells. He suggested that we supplement our diet with a concoction he had made.

His medicine was made by grinding up the brains of calves and soaking them in water and chemicals, then filtering out the solids. We were each given a half gallon and instructed to take three tablespoons per day for six months. Then we were to come back for another series of tests.

The stuff tasted horrible, and some kept it up for only a short time. Others of us took the whole bottle faithfully. After all, it offered some hope. But after the trial period the tests did not produce any conclusive results. Those who had the disease became progressively worse. Another hope was shattered.

Some of the observations we made proved to be interesting. We noticed that the less a muscle was used, the faster it became disabled. Writing became an impossibility for every patient after the disease had progressed for four to eight years. Yet we noticed that my cousin Alice, who loved to crochet and spent most of her time doing so, was able to perform that task quite well even until shortly before her death. Seemingly the constant use of a set of muscles did inhibit the disability to some extent.

Alice had more difficulty than Bert W. in accepting her condition. Neither she nor Aunt Artie could ignore the fact any longer, but they still refused to discuss it very often. Alice loved to play the piano and sing gospel hymns, but slowly lost the ability to do both. She wanted dates, a husband, and a family—and she would have been a good wife and mother—but the disease was already quite evident in her twenties. As the disease progressed she at times became very nervous and apprehensive. Every wedding which involved a member of her peer group caused a new emotional crisis. Dr. Bendix often prescribed a mild sedative which helped her relax and sleep—but he later found that the same result could be obtained with a sugar and salt pill. After Bert W.'s death Alice's condition continued to worsen. She became the victim of recurring attacks of colds and pneumonia. Each time she became weaker and less able to fight a subsequent attack. Aunt Artie was now going through the same heartbreaking experiences with Alice that she had gone through with her husband, my Uncle Will, and Bert W. She shed many tears as she sat at their bedsides, holding their heads as they tried to cough up the mucus from their lungs. She sighed with relief with them when, after the coughing spells had lasted for hours, they were able to clear their throats and breathe freely again. But she knew that in a short time the process would have to be repeated until the cold or pneumonia had run its course.

I knew she spent hours of mental and spiritual anguish, praying as she worked, "Why, Lord, why must they suffer so?"

She must have wondered why my mother was so fortunate, as both of her oldest children were well and apparently would not get ataxia. Yet I never heard her complain about it. I'm certain Aunt Artie knew that my mother's heart ached too as she saw the distress that was their constant companion. These sisters had both gone through the heartrending experience of losing their husbands to ataxia. Together they had prayed and wept and asked God for strength to sustain them when their faith began to waver. Aunt Bertha, their sister, had also lost her husband, Henry, to the disease. She had moved to Iowa shortly after Bert W.'s death, but her letters of encouragement were a source of spiritual strength to all of us. She, too, knew that she might have to go through similar trials with her two sons, Harold and Wilbert, who were still in the risk age.

Amidst all the sickness, we frequently found time to sing together, especially when the cousins were home from college. Wilmena, Aunt Artie's youngest daughter, now in her early twenties, had become a good pianist. She played while we sang the old gospel songs of faith. It was part of our heritage and it helped us to escape some of the present harsh realities and to anticipate the joys beyond sickness and death.

Wilmena was the sweetheart of our group. Her smile was contagious and radiant. She was the most attractive girl in our family and was loved by everybody. She also attended Central College and in a short time attracted several suitors, one of whom she later married.

Many changes had occurred since I had left college in 1934. Hazel and I were married and had two sons. My brother Bert J. was married and established in California. My sister Elsie had gone to California too because work was more plentiful there and because she wanted to escape the stigma of ataxia. My brother John was in college preparing for a medical career. Brother Bill was living with Mom in part of the house we had purchased from her. Bill worked with me on the farm during the summer and at other jobs during the winter.

In Aunt Artie's family, Bert W. had gone to be with the Lord. Alice was home with Aunt Artie. Henry W. was operating the family farm and was apparently well, but there were subtle uncoordinated movements that led us to believe that perhaps he would be the third victim of ataxia in Aunt Artie's family. James had become a pastor after beginning his college career with the intention of becoming a doctor. No doubt there were many factors that changed his mind, but most certainly the faith and courage of his family in the face of adversity was one of the dominant ones. Wilmena too grasped this strong sense of commitment and became a pastor's wife, marrying the Rev. August Tellinghuizen.

Aunt Bertha's son Harold had heard the call to become a minister, as had his father before him; and Wilbert his brother had completed high school and was working near his mother's home in Pella, Iowa.

There were many other cousins in various parts of the country who had either died of ataxia, were ill with it, or were at risk. Their heartaches and problems will not be a part of this record, but I know that sorrow, grief, frustration, distress, and an early death were just as much a part of their lives as they were in our own family.

Two of my Uncle Gerrit Schut's sons, Andrew and John E., came to our community and became a part of our closely knit family. Both were well acquainted with ataxia, as their father and oldest sister had died from it. Several others of their family of nine brothers and sisters were still at risk. Both Andrew and John E. were older than I and were apparently beyond the age of onset. Both had married girls from our community and had homes of their own.

Hazel and I had a very happy relationship, and her understanding and love made my disappointment at not being able to complete my education much easier to accept. She knew my heart ached when my cousins came home from college. Hazel experienced with me some of the joy I had when brother John decided to go into medicine. She also shared some of the financial hardships that were ours as we tried to help him as much as we could. Without her I might have become bitter, but she reminded me that life can be wonderful. I needed only to compare my situation with those who had ataxia. I had a loving wife and two sons, and the Lord was blessing our work on the farm. It seemed that God was answering my prayers—not necessarily as I wanted it but as He willed it.

12

Ataxia Marches On

Ever since that memorable evening in our old home when Pa had said, "That day I shall never see," I had prayed daily that I might be spared the terrible trauma of ataxia. I knew I had no reason to believe that God would hear my prayer any more than those of Bert W. I knew he had prayed as fervently and faithfully as I had, yet God in His all-wise providence had answered, "No, my child, my grace will be your strength to be able to accept your lot in life." And God had certainly done that for him!

I was now thirty-three. The pattern ataxia had taken in our family indicated that if no symptoms appeared by that age I could assume—not with certainty but with a very high probability—that I would be free of the disease and not be able to transmit it to my descendants.

I do not know how or why but suddenly I *knew* that God had answered my prayer affirmatively. That assurance changed our whole outlook toward the future. So many times before both Hazel and I were almost certain I was showing the first symptoms, and we had wept and prayed together that we might receive the grace to face the future. And now, "Praise the Lord," we had the assurance that God had been merciful to us and to our children. Why us and not others? We could not answer that except to see in it a responsibility to those who were still sick and those who would be afflicted in future generations. We knew we could not do much; but what we could do, we would.

In 1943 our first daughter, Marilyn, was born. She was a live wire from birth and a source of great joy.

The farm work kept us very busy. Since so many of the young men had gone to war there was no one available to help with the farm work. Every farmer between eighteen and forty-five was expected to produce a certain amount of farm produce to be eligible for draft deferment. Few farmers had a vacation or day off during the four years of war. It was a small price to pay, of course, compared to those who fought and died in the armed services.

On August 17, 1944, Alice was called home to be with the Lord. She was thirty-seven years old and had suffered from ataxia for fourteen years. She was nearly helpless when death claimed her, the second victim in Aunt Artie's family.

One evening Aunt Artie and her son Henry W. came over to visit Mom. The windows were open and I heard Henry W. cough. It was *that* cough. I had heard it too often to be mistaken.

Did he realize it? Did Aunt Artie suspect it? I was sure that with all the experience they had had with Bert W. and Alice they must know it. I also knew from experience that they would have difficulty admitting it. I did not immediately discuss my suspicions with Henry W. He was much more impulsive and unable to cope with even many of the everyday problems on the farm. How would he cope with ataxia?

World War II had put a complete stop to any work on finding a cure for ataxia, but it proved to be a boon for brother John. Under a government training program, he could receive free medical school education by enlisting in the army. He was having difficulty financing medical school education on his own, so this was a great opportunity. It would mean at least three years before he would have to go into active service, and he would have his degree in three years instead of four. In 1945, shortly after peace was declared, he graduated with honors from the medical school at Northwestern University in Chicago.

The war years brought about many other changes in our family life. Mom had moved to Holland, Michigan, while John attended Hope College there. She kept a boarding house for several college and seminary students besides John, then continued to live in Holland after he entered medical school. Mom was an inspiration to many students as they spent time in her home.

Sister Elsie left California and moved to Holland, where she obtained employment in a factory which made parts for military equipment. Brother Bill also moved to Holland to work in a war plant. For a time Mom, Elsie, John, and Bill were together. These were happy days for Mom. She was busy helping young people and serving the Lord wherever she went. Ataxia still had not made its appearance in her children. She knew, of course, that the probability of her three younger children getting the disease was very real. If she was overly concerned about it, she never indicated it. Her faith in God's providence was so evident in all of her life that she was able to leave even this dreaded possibility in God's hand.

Sister Elsie, now twenty-eight, had had a heartbreaking experience several years earlier when her fiance died from a serious infection. The era of antibiotics had not yet arrived, and infections of many kinds still claimed numerous lives. It took several years for her to recover from that experience.

She fell in love with another young man whom she had met in California. He came to visit her in Holland, and together they made wedding plans and selected furniture for their home. Elsie was on "cloud nine." It proved to be short-lived. Her fiance soon returned to California and never answered Elsie's letters or indicated any interest in her again. Why? Did he detect ataxia symptoms in Elsie? Or was there another reason? I never found out. But the hurt left a permanent scar on Elsie's life. She found several girl friends who also needed companionship. Together this group, who called themselves "The Fifth Wheelers," became a blessing to many in the church and outside it.

Elsie's love for children was almost an obsession, and our children were a special joy to her. Elsie had always said, "I want a lot of children," and had inquired into the possibility of adopting children as a single parent. But the adoption agencies could not even fill the requests that came from couples, so her request was never considered.

Travel by train and bus permitted Mom and Elsie to visit us at different times. On one of her visits to our home I asked Elsie if she would stack the hay as I pitched it up to her from the wagon. The stack became higher as I unloaded the wagon, and Elsie was soon several feet from the ground. I threw the last forkful of hay from the wagon onto the stack. She came near the edge of the stack to climb down to the wagon and I noted a hesitancy as she came close to the edge.

"I don't think I better help you with the next load," she said. "I'm afraid I may fall off the stack."

My thoughts flew. "What makes you think that?" I asked.

She hesitated a moment and looked at me as if to say "You ought to know," but then quietly and calmly said, "Henry, I'm a genuine Schut."

No, Lord, that can't be. My sister, who had been hurt so many times already . . . must she go through the agony of ataxia too?

"I know what you mean," I said. "I've had times when I thought I couldn't balance myself as well as I thought I should. Perhaps you're just tired from the trip yesterday."

"No," she said, "I've noticed it for some time already. I know I have the disease."

I tried to think of something to say.

"I know it isn't much comfort, but we all must face death sooner or later."

She looked at me and said, "It isn't death I'm afraid of, but what I have to go through before death. After all, there are worse things to face than death—you ought to know that by now."

"Yes, but are you sure you have ataxia? There are other people who have problems with walking."

"I know I have it," she insisted.

When Elsie "knew" something you didn't argue. It was a waste of time. Besides that, I noticed the characteristic wandering of her hand as she reached out to my hand as I helped her down from the haystack. I watched her walk toward the house. Yes, there was no doubt about it. My heart hurt and I wept. Another dear one must die inches at a time.

As soon as I had an opportunity I discussed it with Hazel. She had also observed the symptoms of ataxia in Elsie. A helpless feeling came over me as I thought of Elsie's future. There just wasn't one thing I could do. It was as if she were drowning in the middle of the ocean and I had no way of rescuing her. The only difference was that death by drowning would be quick.

The secret (such as it was) was out. We talked freely with Elsie about her future plans. She would continue to work at her job in Holland as long as the company permitted her to do so, and Mom would stay with her.

Elsie seemed to accept very nonchalantly the future that lay ahead. "Whatever will be, will be. I'll do the best I can and leave the rest to the Lord." She asked for no pity and was determined not to be a burden to anyone. She had somehow managed to inherit my father's determination and independence without getting his hot temper.

I had now seen at close hand the reaction of four people to ataxia. Pa could not accept it and reacted in anger and frustration. Bert W. accepted his lot with patience and calm serenity. Alice tried her best to ignore her handicaps. Now Elsie responded with resignation, but with a determination that her life would still be meaningful and useful. One thing they all had in common was an assurance that God controlled every aspect of their lives and that what He did was good, even though they couldn't always understand how.

"Be still, and know that I am God," my mother quoted frequently. How do you receive a faith like that? I knew and believed in a personal God, but to calmly accept the burdens that He seemed to indiscriminately lay on people wasn't easy for me to do. Yes, I was thankful that I had been spared, but standing by these loved ones as they struggled to walk; as they tried to talk so people could understand; as they fought for their breath, choking and nearly suffocating, caused me inwardly to cry out, "Why, God, why?"

In 1946 our second daughter, Darlene, came into our home, a happy lovable girl—one more reason for us to thank God and count our blessings. Now there were six of us. Life for Hazel and me was busy but filled with love.

And I was healthy.

13

"Why Me, O God?"

Henry W. (or Henk as we called him most often) and I were sitting outside by Aunt Artie's one Sunday evening when he suddenly turned toward me.

"Tell me something," he said. "Do you think I have ataxia?"

"Sometimes I think you do and sometimes I'm not sure," I answered evasively. I stopped a moment and continued, "You do have that cough, and it scares me."

"Well," he said, "I'm sure I have it. I stumble a lot and I can't write as well as I could. I can't hit a nail with a hammer very well, and many things are hard for me to do."

"There were times I thought I couldn't do things as well as others could," I said, "but later on I would see others make the same mistakes I did."

"Oh," he answered, "you don't have it. That's sure. You are better coordinated and quicker than almost anyone I know."

Henk continued in a rather bitter voice, "First, brother Bert, then sister Alice, and now me. Why, oh, why, does God have to pick on three of us in a row? I want to live. I want to have a wife. I want children. Why must I be denied all those? And on top of all that, I'll have to suffer just like Bert and Alice. What about my mother? Hasn't

95

she had enough grief already? Must she take care of me for years and years too? It isn't fair! God isn't fair!" Tears of anger, frustration, and bitterness rolled down his face. "Why me, Henry, why me?"

I wasn't prepared for this outburst, but I could really feel for him. I waited a moment to answer because I didn't know what to say.

"I can't answer your question because I don't have an answer," I finally said. "I could ask, 'Why *not* me, oh, Lord?' There just are some things that have no acceptable answer in this life. All I know is I do believe that, somehow, God is doing what is best."

"That's easy for you to say—everything is going your way."

"I know that, but I want you to know that when you hurt, I hurt too. I prayed, too, that you would be well, but God has said No. Why? I don't have the answer, that's sure."

"I get so frustrated," Henk continued. "This job of farming is getting so hard. The cows get through the fence, and I can't fix it up the way it should be because I can't get the wires tight. The hogs get out and I can't run fast enough to get ahead of them. I spill a lot of milk because I can't control my hands. Everything I do takes longer. I can't get the field work done on time, so the crop yield isn't as good as it ought to be. Everything seems to be going wrong. What am I going to do?"

It was the same problem I had seen with my father. I had no real answer—because there was none.

"I think we can get some of the neighbors to help put in some of the crops, and I'll try to help some too," I replied.

"But how long can that go on? I won't get any better. If I would be sick for only a short time, then I could manage with the neighbors' help, but not indefinitely."

"I know that," I said, "but that's the only way. Your brother Jim can't be expected to come home."

"I'd never ask him to leave the ministry to help us. I'm happy for him, and perhaps a little jealous. He's nearly thirty years old and doesn't seem to have any symptoms yet. Perhaps he, at least, won't be affected. I'm surely praying for that."

We talked at length about the future. I asked him, "Do you know that Elsie is also showing signs?"

"Yes, I noticed it the last time she was home. How does she feel about it?"

"She just says, 'That's the way it is,' and lets it go at that. I'm sure she hurts more than she is willing to admit. But you know Elsie. She won't accept any pity. She's determined to make it on her own as long as she can."

"I wish I had some of her attitude," he replied wistfully. "I know it's tough on Mom when I get so angry and bitter. But I think she feels like I do at times. She can't understand either why she must face ataxia in the first three of her children. But she seems to be able to get strength from her faith in the infinite wisdom of God. I just rebel against that idea. I can't accept it, and I won't!"

"I'm afraid I can't be of much help to you. Only *you* can change your attitude, and you will be unhappy and bitter until you do."

"But you and Bert J. don't realize what it's like to really *know* that you can't live a normal life," he said. "People with other diseases may have a faint hope for a cure, but I don't have any. There's nothing to live for. I'd be much better off if I were killed tomorrow. At least I wouldn't have to die a little every day."

What could I say? How *would* I feel if I had a future like Henk's?

We went into the house where Aunt Artie and Hazel were visiting. After a short time Hazel, our children, and I went home. I never appreciated my family and my health so much as I did that evening.

There was something different about the way ataxia affected Henk. As time went on I noticed the characteristic handicaps, but the progress was much slower. Perhaps it was his stubborn will to live.

During Henk's bouts with colds he became very apprehensive. He often got chills, or the "shakes" as he called them. His entire body shook and the bed vibrated with him. Fear gripped him and he really thought he was going to die. Aunt Artie often called Dr. Bendix, who came and assured Henk that death was not imminent. A very compassionate physician, he always took time out to talk.

There were other times when Aunt Artie did not want to call Dr. Bendix. Then Henk became angry and convulsed with chills. Quite often Aunt Artie reached her wits' end and called me or a neighbor. I would go to their home, massage his shaking body, and speak reassuringly to him. Sometimes aspirin and glass of hot milk helped calm him down. Often he would blurt out the same unanswerable question we had discussed before: "Why do I have to have this disease? Why?"

He would pound the bed clothes and throw the pillows on the floor. Aunt Artie would remonstrate, but he would shout, "You don't know what it's like not to be able to walk right. You can't feel my feelings! Nobody can!"

"I do too, Henk," she quietly replied one day, with tears streaming down her cheeks. "My heart aches more than you can ever know. I don't know either why you must suffer so."

Frequently after an outburst like that he would calm down and say, "I'm sorry I became so angry," then drop off to sleep.

One occasion stands out in my memory. Henk had caught a cold and was in bed with one of his shaking spells. Aunt Artie had been up with him so many times during the previous nights that she was exhausted. She called and asked if I could sit up with Henk. It was already late in the evening when I walked into the house unannounced. As I walked into the bedroom I stopped short. Aunt Artie had changed into her nightgown and was on her knees beside the bed.

I stepped quietly back into the living room. This moment was sacred; I could not disturb it. What power, what faith, did this woman possess? She had spent nearly thirty years watching first her husband, then her two oldest children die of this disease. Now when her third child was following the same inevitable pattern she still had the faith to drop her exhausted body to its knees. What she prayed I do not know, but I'm sure she was asking God, if possible, that He would still heal her son. My memory flew back to that hospital room twenty years before, where my mother knelt beside my bed and asked God to heal her son. God had graciously answered her petition. But what possible hope was there that God would heal Henk?

It soon became apparent that Henk would not be able to operate the farm. He tried so hard, but there was no way the farm could support them. Nothing seemed to go right. The cows didn't give much milk, the machinery broke down, and the crops didn't produce a normal yield—mostly because Henk could not perform the work that had to be done. The danger of having an accident with the machinery or livestock finally forced Aunt Artie to sell the farm and move to a small home in Silver Creek.

All during the illnesses of Aunt Artie's family, many friends and relatives gave assistance and comfort. Without this help it would have been impossible for her to carry her load. When Aunt Artie moved to Silver Creek this concern continued. Two persons stand out in particular. Aunt Artie's cousin, William Mol, with his wife Gertrude, were available day or night. Gertrude seemed to be able to tolerate Henk's angry outbursts, and he learned to appreciate her. She lived only a block away, and every time she left she would say, "I'll see you tomorrow."

Many times Henk refused to take his medicine or get out of bed to exercise. No amount of coaxing by Aunt Artie would make him change his mind, so Gertrude would go to work on him.

"What's the use?" he would say. "I can't get better anyway."

"Yes," Gertrude would tell him. "That may be true. But you'll become completely disabled much sooner if you don't try to walk. Then you won't be able to get out of bed at all."

Reluctantly he would let them help him dress, and he would walk behind a metal walking frame they had purchased for him.

At the time Aunt Artie moved to Silver Creek we became acquainted with Dr. Raetz. He was a general practitioner in Maple Lake, a town closer than Annandale and on the same telephone exchange as Silver Creek. He showed the same concern that Dr. Bendix did and frequently stopped in without being called to check on Henk's health. Words cannot express the gratitude we owe to these two doctors. They were helpless to cure ataxia; but their interest, concern, and genuine love in our time of need made the burden much lighter.

Meanwhile, brother John had graduated from medical school and was serving his country in the army. The war was over, but the army expected him to serve two years to compensate the government for putting him through school. His brilliant mind and his interest in neurology opened up the opportunity to be assigned to the Army Institute of Pathology in Washington, D.C. He was assigned to work on research in neurology, and he was overjoyed. He wrote me: "What an act of Providence! First God provides me with a free medical education, and now He puts me here where I can work on ataxia. I'm sure He has a purpose in all this: perhaps I can find a cure for this terrible disease."

On April 15, 1948, Linda and Lois, our twin daughters, came into our home. Life never was the same after that. There had been considerable activity and motion before their arrival, but now it was constant.

14

One Man's Fight

Brother John was a born fighter, and when he made a decision to do something he put everything he had into it. He was twenty-six when he started his research work on ataxia. During his medical school training we kept up correspondence, but now that he was assigned to work full time on ataxia we kept up a steady flow of letters.

He wrote about his work, his findings and theories about ataxia, and asked me to respond to them. He asked me to watch Henk and to report every detail of the course of the disease in his life. He sent me reprints of articles written by other doctors throughout the world, explaining them in laymen's terms. Nowhere in the literature that brother John read did ataxia seem to take such a distinct pattern as with the Schut-Vanden Berg family; and nowhere else did it attack such a large family.

John also asked me to help bring the family tree up to date, indicating the age of onset, age àt death, and many other pertinent facts. He correlated all these facts and wrote several articles on ataxia which were published in medical research journals all over the world.

One of the difficulties with ataxia was that it was a comparatively uncommon and unknown disease. John thought that a film showing the victims of the disease and describing the tests as they were performed on the patients would be helpful to doctors and medical schools. He was able to obtain funds to produce a forty-five-minute sound film showing how to diagnose ataxia. It was filmed in our community and in other places in the midwest. The film was helpful in providing publicity and in aiding physicians to differentiate between ataxia and multiple sclerosis and other similar diseases.

Dr. John (as he was soon called by the relatives) became well known by neurologists throughout the area. He found ataxia families not related to ours and tried to get them to help in the fight against it. But Dr. John could not understand how some people felt and could not tolerate families keeping the disease a secret. He would say, "You can't fight a disease that is kept in a closet. Let's get it out in the open. It's nothing to be ashamed of." He had a deep concern for the health of people, but lacked the tact and diplomacy necessary to win them to his way of thinking. He spent time and money to help people in need, but could be very blunt if they refused to follow his advice.

Shortly after his graduation Dr. John had married a girl he had met during his stay in Northwestern Medical School in Chicago. Not wishing to risk passing the disease on to the next generation, he had had himself sterilized before he was married. Mom, Elsie, and I were able to attend both the graduation and the wedding. We thought John had made a good choice, but John's personality made the marriage a stormy one.

During his army service Dr. John discovered that there appeared to be an excessive amount of a certain chemical in the spinal fluid of ataxia victims—a discovery that corroborated Dr. Rossen's research several years before. He could not explain why, but theorized that it was due to the destruction of the nerve cells in the brain, which then left a larger than normal amount of this chemical as a residue. Out of this he developed two theories.

One was that the gene controlling the metabolism of some type of food chemical was either absent or defective. If this chemical was needed to nourish the nerve cells in the brain, its absence could cause a nerve cell to die. This in turn would cause connecting nerve cells to die from disuse. Research had revealed extensive damage to all the parts of the brain that control movement, but much lesser damage to the parts which control thinking and decision-making. The question was: Where was the primary culprit?

The second theory was that a defective gene caused a toxin or poison to be formed. This caused the destruction of the primary nerve cells, which in turn triggered a "domino effect" on surrounding cells.

Obviously it would be very useful to be able to examine the brain of a victim who was showing the first symptoms of ataxia. But this possibility was very remote. It could only be done in the case of accidental death.

The more we delved into these theories and studied the possibilities of their being true, the more complicated the situation became. Where should we begin? If indeed a toxin was formed, what was it and where did it come from? We knew of one disease in which the body was unable to eliminate the minute quantities of copper that are found in the normal diet. The build-up of copper caused a disease called Wilson's disease. We also knew that diabetes is usually caused by the inability of the body to produce insulin, which is needed to burn up sugar.

Dr. John spent months studying literature on ataxia from all over the world. It became almost an obsession with him. Most of the literature described the symptoms, genetic pattern, and pathology of the disease; but very little research had been done to find a cure. The function of each part of the brain was known to a limited degree, but how the nerve cells received their nourishment was still not clearly known.

Dr. John thought a drug named Glutamicol might be useful in supplying nourishment for the nerve cells. He used another drug named Niacin, which was supposed to dilate the blood vessels so the Glutamicol could reach the nerve cells better. He obtained the drugs and sent them to six cousins who had the disease. The drug did seem to help some of the victims temporarily, but after six months there was no permanent regression of the disease. It was a great disappointment.

After trying several different drugs, we noticed that there often seemed to be some improvement for a short time, regardless of the drug. Dr. John explained it by reporting, "There is an element of psychosomatic illness connected with ataxia."

Dr. John believed there was a definite degeneration of the cerebrum, the thinking part of the brain. He had found some changes, he said, in the cerebra of those who had died of the disease. He even indicated that these changes might be the first phase of the degenerative process.

"This idea that the mind is not affected is comforting to us," he said. "We, as a family, don't want to have a disease in which there is mental deterioration. But I've examined enough patients to know that this idea of there being no mental change is pure poppycock."

"But how do you determine," I asked, "whether the mental change is due to a degeneration of the cerebrum or to the person's reaction to the disease? After all, anyone who can't even talk or walk well when in the prime of life is likely to act irrationally at times."

My thoughts went back to the time when Pa had taken his shotgun and shot one of his cows. That certainly wasn't a rational act. Was it due to a degeneration of the cerebrum or to the utter frustration of not being able to fix the fence well enough to keep the cows in?

The pressure to find a cure became intense. Henk was severely affected, and sister Elsie was becoming more and more helpless. Now there seemed to be the beginning symptoms in cousin Wilmena. And at times I was suspicious of some of the actions of my brother Bill. I recalled the evening when several of us boys were having a one-legged race. We invited Bill to compete, but he refused. "I can't run well in that kind of race," he said. The statement didn't strike me as being unusual at the time, but the next day I began to wonder.

Dr. John never forgot that he was still in the risk age. I quote from a letter he wrote in 1949 when he was twenty-eight years old and working in the Army Institute of Pathology, Washington, D.C.:

Last week when I thought I had proved the possibility of MN linkage to myself and had drawn some conclusions as to my fate therefrom, I really felt blue for some time. It is not only that, Henry, but there are other little things which cause me to fear that I am a future victim. It is not that these symptoms and signs are constant, but they are intermittent, just like they are supposed to be in the first stages. Now today is the best day that I've had for a time, but it will come back—difficulty in pronouncing certain words, *that* cough, loss of weight, correct age, and large pupils. My reflexes are becoming more active I believe, and I have a pendulous patellar reflex like Elsie has. But I do not have trouble with walking, and in fact, I walk better with my eyes closed than open.

You see I am trying to prevent what happened to Alice, who could hardly walk without a cane before she admitted the possibility to herself. But on the other hand, I fully realize the implications of forming the opposite conclusion too quickly, and thus have shoved it from my mind for some time.

These little signs that I have—I do not know their significance yet. I am so anxious to examine some-one who has passed through the same age period and ask them if they noted similar symptoms that *disappeared entirely.* I can recall distinctly that cousin Harold talked with a definite slur on his voice when in Chicago. However, I talked with him over the phone recently and am convinced that he shall remain free forever. Possibly that was a transient sign which dis-appeared. If so, that will be of tremendous value to me and to others and to the understanding of the disease too. I cannot cough like others. Why? Possibly others have a controlling factor which keeps the rest of the disease in abeyance. You can visualize the importance of this, for the study of these controlling factors will constitute a valuable way in which to find out the cause of the disease as well as the gene's mechanism of action.

One time you told me that you thought you were going to get it for sure. You can do me a great service, Henry, by writing me and telling me what symptoms you noted. You see, you will serve as the great control for Billy and me when I come to Minneapolis. Elsie has something which you didn't get, and which Bill and I may get. Therefore let's study us four, to see if we can come to any conclusions. Of course we are handicapped because Elsie is of the opposite sex. But, on the other hand, we know that this disease has noth-ing to do with sex, for both sexes get it. It is something besides sex and the secondary sex characteristics which causes it.

I will close this letter now. Of course there is much here that must needs not go outside thine portals. Let no one know that I entertain these fears, for it will do no good for the cause for which I have devoted my life.

Respectfully,

John

I went back over some of the letters Dr. John had typed to me several years before and noted a definite increase in the mistakes he made. Could this indicate a beginning of the lack of coordination that was so characteristic of ataxia, or did it indicate that he was very busy and more in a hurry? I had not seen him for a year, and at that time his walking and talking seemed normal. I wanted to see him. But I dreaded it, lest I would see and hear the symptoms that would sentence him to only ten years to live.

15

Time Is Running Out

Dr. John was discharged from the army in 1949 when he was twenty-nine years old. While in the army he had written several articles on ataxia, directed a forty-five-minute sight-sound production on how to diagnose the disease, tried different medications on many different patients, and accumulated much information on ataxia from sources throughout the world. He now realized that he must have more training and study in neurology, the study of the nervous system. He applied for and was accepted as a resident at the University of Minnesota at Minneapolis. This was a three- or four-year program, after which a student could take an examination. If he passed it, he would become a certified neurologist. Dr. John entered this program with his characteristic determination, and he succeeded in receiving his certificate in neurology.

During the time of his residency at the university the disease had progressed in our sister Elsie to the extent that she could no longer be employed in the shop where she worked. She and Mom decided to return from Michigan to Silver Creek, where they built a new home not far from Aunt Artie and Henk.

Said Elsie in her characteristic stoical manner, "Yes, I'm coming back to Minnesota to die. Then I can be buried with the rest of those who died of our disease."

She wanted no pity. Still able to walk, she refused to use a cane. "If I fall, I'll just get up again or crawl," she replied to those who wanted her to use some type of support.

The disease progressed much more rapidly in Elsie than it did in cousin Henk. That was not unusual, as there seemed to be modifying factors in some people. These could deter the progress of the disease or cause it to affect some parts of the body more severely than others. Elsie was much more handicapped in her speech and hands than was Henk. But Elsie could walk, which Henk was unable to do.

Dr. John predicted that if Elsie contracted pneumonia she would have difficulty coughing and be unable to expel the mucus from her lungs. She would probably die from suffocation as Pa and cousin Bert W. had done. It wasn't a pleasant thought, but there was one redeeming factor. The victims who were affected this way never lived long enough to become completely disabled. This seems like a heartless statement, but the distress and handicaps that were a part of ataxia were so difficult to face that a shorter life was often more desirable. I knew Elsie would find it very difficult to cope with nearly total disability. Dr. John came out to visit her often, as it was only fifty miles from his work. Frequently he brought along different medications for her to take. But it was to no avail. The disease continued its relentless course.

Dr. John was now studying neurology, and the more he learned about ataxia the more frustrated he became. He learned the immensity of the problem. There were literally thousands of possible causes for ataxia symptoms, and it was impossible to isolate and try the hundreds of different chemicals that might treat the specific cause. It would be pure chance if he were to find the right combination. He took every course in chemistry and biology he could and read every article on ataxia he could find. He discovered a cat that had ataxia and studied its brain thoroughly. He wrote many letters to me asking questions about my observations of ataxia victims. I would answer, giving some of my theories, which he would study and either refute or corroborate.

One day Dr. John came to our home, as he often did. "Henry," he said, "the other day I went to the cafe and ordered my lunch and a cup of coffee. As I was carrying my tray, the coffee cup slid around on my tray. I couldn't control my hands well enough to stop the cup from sliding first one way and then another. I watched in sheer terror and said right out loud, 'Oh, no, God. I've got the disease!'"

I had been watching him at different times ever since he had returned to Minnesota. At times I was certain he had the first symptoms, and at other times he seemed to be well coordinated; but I also knew that this was the usual pattern of the disease. After a year or more the symptoms would remain.

I couldn't say anything for some time. What could I say? "I'm not sure," I hedged. "Sometimes I think you have the first symptoms and at other times I don't see them."

"Well, I'm sure," he said bitterly. "What do I do now? My time to find a cure is limited. I was so sure that God was leading me all through my life so I would be able to help these poor people. Now I'm beginning to feel that God is letting me down."

"You still have some years before you are helpless. Perhaps you can still find a cure," I said.

"That may be true, but I get so frustrated, and now it looks like my marriage is going to break up. We're constantly fighting."

"You never were easy to live with," I told him bluntly.

"I know that," he said. "I even get in trouble with my professors and superiors in the university, but no one knows the pressure I'm under. I'm going to run out of time."

111

"You better learn to live with your wife," I told him. "You may need her."

"That's just the problem. I don't think she will be able to cope with the problems ataxia will bring."

"That depends a lot on your attitude toward life and toward her."

"That's possible, but I'm just at the point in my training where I can do something. If I pass the exam, I have a job in the state hospital waiting for me. I can work on research there while I am on the job. It's a beautiful setup. Now it seems the whole thing is falling down like a house of cards. It's difficult to keep a good attitude toward anything or anybody."

"I know it's difficult to be patient," I said. "You and I are both impatient persons. We can't wait for anything or anybody, not even God. But I know He can reveal a cure to you if it's His will."

"It's easy for you to give me that pious stuff; everything's going your way."

I acknowledged that, but I also pointed out that I was doing everything I could to help the others in our families who had ataxia.

"You sure are lucky," he kept on. "If you had ataxia, three of your six children would probably get it too."

"You may be sure that if I had had the disease when I was thirty, we wouldn't have had that many."

"Too bad Pa and Ma didn't stop having children when he got the disease," said John. "Then I wouldn't have been born." He turned and walked away.

There was little doubt about it. He was swaying as he walked. I turned around and walked to the barn with a prayer of gratitude in my heart that I could walk straight, and a prayer that Dr. John would receive from God the ability to face the future.

Not long afterward John and his wife were divorced.

Little brother Bill had also grown up. He returned from Holland, Michigan, to work on the farm for Uncle Arnold Vandergon. This entitled him to a draft deferment.

Bill was a popular young man and had dated many girls. He never became serious about marriage, however, until Dorothy worked for us for a short time while Hazel was not well.

The serious impact ataxia has on its victims and their families cannot be realized by an occasional encounter with a victim, but Dorothy saw a lot of Elsie and Henk and heard the story of "Schut's disease." She asked me, "Do you think Bill will get the disease your cousin Henk and your sister Elsie have?"

How was I to answer her? I loved this brother, who was so different from the rest of our family. He was as much a son to me as he was a brother. If I truthfully told Dorothy that my twenty-year-old brother could very well be a victim, I would undoubtedly destroy any chance Bill had of marrying the girl he loved. Yet I couldn't say No, because he was still at risk. The dilemma I faced was heartrending.

Finally I said, "I don't know. Bill is still too young for me to say Yes or No."

"But what do you think?" she pressed.

"There are times I think he shows some symptoms—but I had what I thought were symptoms too when I was his age. Now I know they had no significance because I'm past the risk age. All I can say is that my father lived a normal life until the last five or six years of his life. We had a happy home until he became ill. And his symptoms occurred later in his life than they did in the lives of his brothers or sisters. So it may be that the disease hits our particular family at an older age. But, no, that isn't true either, because Elsie isn't thirty years old yet. She has followed the normal pattern of showing first symptoms in the twenties and becoming progressively disabled."

Dorothy looked thoughtfully into the distance. I searched for words to help her in the hard decision she was facing. Bill deserved to be considered as a husband; yet I wouldn't want to encourage her to marry a man who might die young after years of disability.

"There is one thing I do know," I continued. "You don't get a fifty-year guarantee with any man. I know Bill will be a good provider, and he has always been very considerate and kind to our mother. That is usually a good criteria by which to judge a man as a husband."

"I don't know what to do! I love him, but it scares me to think I might be marrying a man who will become an invalid, and even worse, that we might have children who might be afflicted as well. But still, Bill might not get it at all. After all, you didn't."

"I can't make your decision for you," I said. "I know how difficult it is, though. Just ten years ago Hazel and I were in the same position as you and Bill are now."

She turned away with tears in her eyes. "I'll have to pray and think about it some more," she said.

I was happy—and afraid—when they announced not long afterward that they had set their wedding date.

After Bill and Dorothy were married he quit working for my uncle and thereby lost his draft deferment. Although the war was over, he was drafted into the army and sent to Japan to serve in the occupation forces. He was one of those selected to be honor guard for General Douglas Mac-Arthur. Less than two years after being drafted, he returned home and started to farm for himself in 1947. We often helped each other with the planting and harvesting.

Bill was now twenty-five years old. Occasionally he coughed—was it "that" cough, the dreaded cough that had brought fear to my heart before? After a while I could no longer evade the issue. Did Bill realize it? I didn't know.

He was a very private person and didn't reveal his feelings openly.

One day I asked him, "Bill, do you and Dorothy plan to have children before you're thirty? You know you're still at risk."

"I want children," he replied, "and I don't want to wait till I'm thirty to have them."

We had had our first son when I was only twenty-six and still at risk, yet I cautioned him, "I surely don't think a person should have children if he knows or suspects he has ataxia!"

"Oh, I don't know," he countered, "that's a personal matter, and each person should be allowed to decide that for himself."

I didn't want to press the issue. I knew that Dr. John had made his views known to Bill in no uncertain terms. We never spoke of it again. Bill made it clear that the issue was not open for discussion, and I had no choice but to accept it.

In 1948, Bill and Dorothy had a son. He was a source of joy to all of us. What the future would bring for him only God knew, and I was content to leave the matter in His hand.

Elsie and Mom moved into their new home in 1951 and were soon settled into a new routine. Mom was now sixty-eight years old, and Elsie thirty-six. Ataxia had affected the muscles in Elsie's throat quite severely. There were few meals during which she did not choke on something. It seemed that the muscles that were supposed to close the opening to her lungs did not work properly, and food got into her windpipe. To make matters worse, it was difficult for her to cough, and at times she became blue before she dislodged the piece of food. It was a frightening experience, and Elsie came to dread each meal.

In October of 1953, Elsie caught a severe cold. Her

115

coughing spells became so severe and prolonged that we decided to take her to the hospital. We wanted to carry her to the car, but she insisted on walking. As she did so she held her outstretched arms to each side like a balancing pole. I marveled at her determination. Dr. Raetz immediately put Elsie on antibiotics, and she responded quickly. Mom, Dr. John, and I went to the hospital the morning her temperature returned to normal. When we arrived we saw that her condition was still critical. She could only say one word at a time. She was trying to cough, but was unable to eliminate very much mucus. Dr. John felt that the mucus would have a better chance to come out if Elsie's head were lowered, so I held her head and pounded her on the back. The mucus did come out as far as the throat, but she couldn't bring it up. We tried to use washcloths and our fingers. The mucus was draining out of her lungs into her throat, and she could hardly get air into her lungs. She became frantic.

"Up!" she cried. "Up!"

"Elsie," I said, "That stuff must get out. You can't cough it up, so we are trying to let it run out."

"Up! Up!" Elsie yelled.

She began to throw herself around in a frantic effort to get air.

I turned up the bed so she could sit up. She relaxed a bit, but the terror of the last few minutes remained in her eyes. She was exhausted and put her head back on the pillow.

Dr. John had asked for an aspirating machine as soon as we came. When it arrived he and the nurse began to get it hooked up. I decided to watch them work on it. They had the machine just about ready when I glanced toward Elsie and Mom. Mom beckoned to me to come.

"I believe Elsie is unconscious," Mom said. "Her eyes look like she doesn't see anything."

I looked at Elsie's face and shouted, "John, she's quit breathing!"

Dr. John flew into action. The aspirator was ready.

He opened her limp jaws and jammed the suction tube down her throat. She gagged a few times and lay still.

Dr. John was furious with himself.

"She's dead!" he cried, "and I've failed!"

Mom was still holding Elsie's hand. Tears were rolling down her face. "Lord," she prayed, "she is with You now, and Your will be done."

"Mom," John said, "I don't believe that it was God's will that Elsie should die. It's my fault. I should have come sooner and got this aspirator going."

"No, it's not your fault," I said. "You did all you could, and besides I think it's much better this way. Elsie would not want to be completely helpless. She has enjoyed life this far, and now that her body can't do what she wants it to do, God called her home."

"It isn't right," he returned. "It isn't fair! You can't tell me Elsie didn't want to live. Everybody wants to live, no matter how sick or disabled they are."

"I can't wish her back even though my heart aches," said Mom. "She's with the Lord and in a much happier place. Her future is now beautiful."

"What's the problem?" Dr. Raetz asked as he came running into the room.

"I've failed," said Dr. John as he broke into sobs.

"Why, what happened?" he asked.

"She suffocated," John said. "We could have performed a tracheotomy and aspirated her lungs through the opening, but it's too late now."

"What would have happened to the hole if she became well again?" Mom asked.

John explained that a curved metal tube would have been inserted in the hole. This could be taken out, cleaned, and put back. To talk, she would have had to place her finger over the hole. She would have had to live with it the rest of her life, and would have needed an aspirator in her home. "At the most," said Dr. Raetz, "it would have added two or three years to her life."

"I think it's better this way," said Mom.

It had been a little less than ten years since she had helped me stack hay and said, "I'm a genuine Schut."

We buried her in the family plot next to Pa.

There was room for four graves in the plot. Two were still vacant. We knew Mom wanted to lie in one of them. "That leaves one for me," cried Dr. John, "but I'm going to fight to the last breath to stay out of it. You can bet on that!"

He remained generally well and was able to carry on his work without much difficulty. There were times, however, when he had some difficulty walking, especially if he was tired or under tension. On one such occasion he walked up the sidewalk to visit a patient. The door suddenly opened and a man called out, "Don't you come in here! We don't want a drunk doctor in the house!"

He never forgot that incident. He knew now that he could not practice medicine anywhere unless the community knew he was handicapped.

Having been divorced from his first wife, he now re-married. Mary Reisdorfer knew he had ataxia but had absolute faith that he would find a cure before he died from it. I did not share her optimism. I noticed slight indications that he could not think as well, especially in the area of innovative ideas and theories. His brilliant mind was being affected, either by the disease itself or by the emotional impact of having to face a nearly hopeless future. But he would never admit the hopelessness of his task; he just *knew* he would find a cure.

The urgency of finding a cure became ever more pressing. Brother Bill definitely had the disease, cousin Henk was nearly helpless, and cousin Wilmena was severely affected. Besides, there were many other first and second cousins in other parts of the country who were in various stages of the disease. Now the very person we had all hoped could find a cure was himself a victim.

I had not lost all hope, but realized that the prospect of finding a cure in the next ten years was certainly dim. Perhaps if an all-out research program could be financed, there might be a possibility. But the disease was comparatively rare, and not enough people were affected to arouse the necessary interest.

The future for these loved ones looked grim, but there was one person who did not fear the future. I told Mom, "It looks like time is running out for our family."

"What's time," she asked, "when you compare it to eternity? That's where we will spend most of our existence anyway, so why worry about time running out?"

16

What's the Use of Fighting?

Time had indeed run out for Elsie. After her death I went through a period of despair. I had lived and worked with ataxia for over thirty years. Pa and Elsie were gone, cousin Bert and cousin Alice were gone, and cousins Henk and Wilmena were so severely affected that it would be only a few years before they would be gone. Even if a cure were found, would those who had it recover the use of their bodily functions? Would someone like Henk have to live a normal life span without being able to dress or feed himself? That possibility seemed worse than death. The common opinion among the doctors was that once a nerve cell is destroyed it can never again be replaced or renewed. The doctors performed an autopsy on Elsie, and found gross destruction of many parts of the cerebellum and other parts of the nearby nervous system. These parts could not be restored. Of what value would a cure be to those severely handicapped?

I shared this with Dr. John. He was horrified by my attitude.

"Listen, Henry," he said, "Bill and I are still quite well. I would be happy if I could find something that would stop this hellish disease in my body right where it is. I could lead a nearly normal life and so could Bill. For another thing, there are still hundreds of children in the risk age."

"It seems such a hopeless task," I replied.

"Henry, you can't quit now. I need you worse than ever, and if you don't give me your support, I *am* in a hopeless situation."

"But I've spent so much time, money, and energy over the last twenty-five years trying to help, and now we are no closer to a cure than we were then."

"No, we don't have a cure, but we have learned a lot. We have spread the knowledge of ataxia to hundreds of doctors and thousands of people. By using antibiotics we can keep ataxia victims alive an average of two or three years longer."

"Just two or three years more of living death. What gain is that?"

He ignored my question and continued. "Medical research is discovering new facts every day. It just takes one correct theory and we may be on the road to a cure."

Then he went on to tell me about a number of other hereditary diseases that are similar to ataxia. There were, for instance, several people in the state hospital who had Huntington's disease. It has the same genetic pattern as the Schut ataxia, but the victims have many bizarre motions they cannot control. They become mentally and physically handicapped over a period of years. Some become affected when they are around forty and fifty years old, and they often live many years after they get the first symptoms. It's a terrible disease, and most of the time they have a family before they know they are going to become affected. That means that they are at risk a much longer time. The only way to eliminate the disease is to eliminate the family line.

"I'm convinced," said Dr. John, "that if we find a cure for ataxia we will also have some clues as to how to cure these other hereditary nerve diseases. You see, Henry, the future of many families is at stake, so I plan to put everything I've got into this work."

His job at the state hospital in Anoka, Minnesota, was more demanding than he had thought it would be, however, and he and Mary decided to go to Galesburg, Illinois, where the state hospital would give him more opportunity for research.

Henk continued to have repeated bouts with colds and pneumonia, but since his diaphragm was not seriously affected he was able to expel the mucus from his lungs. With antibiotics that were now available he was able to recover. But every bout left him weaker and more handicapped. He became very irritable and at times irrationally angry, lashing out in frustration at whoever happened to be near—which was usually his mother. Fortunately, with the help of neighbors and my mother, Aunt Artie was able to cope with the situation. Some people suggested the possibility of having Henk put in a state institution, but she would not consider it. She insisted that the Lord would continue to give her strength. Somehow He did.

A short time after Elsie's death our church was without a permanent pastor, and we were served by a retired pastor, the Rev. Matthew Duven. His vast experience and his strong faith made him a perfect person to counsel with Henk. He made it a point to visit Henk regularly, and slowly but surely I noticed a change in Henk's attitude.

Mr. Duven was able to persuade Henk to consider God's promises that He is ever near to them that seek Him. He told Henk that he could conquer bitterness and anger if he would surrender his life and will to the Lord. Contentment and acceptance of his lot in life could be found if he would just permit God to take over. It was difficult. Henk was now forty-one years old and had been denied health, a home of his own, a wife, children, and a means of livelihood; everything, in fact, that makes life worth living. To be able to say, "Yes, Lord, I accept Your will for my life" would take a miracle of God's grace. After weeks of counseling and prayer, the miracle happened. He became convinced that his life still had meaning and that the purposes of God could be fulfilled in him. Mr. Duven left our church after serving us just six months, but it proved to be the turning point in Henk's life.

This made life much easier for Aunt Artie, but the burden of caring for Henk was still heavy. In 1954 he began to get periods of uremic poisoning, indicating that his kidneys were not functioning well. Dr. Raetz told us there was very little that could be done. We could take him to the hospital, but that would merely prolong a condition which would inevitably take his life. Aunt Artie decided to take care of him at home and let God decide when He wanted to take him to his eternal home.

Slowly the bodily functions ceased and Henk went into a coma. Early one morning he quietly slipped out of his helpless body to a place where there is no disease, no bitterness, and no sorrow. Henk's death was so different from that of the others I had seen—no choking, no terror, no struggle—just the quiet exchange of the temporal life for the eternal.

Aunt Artie was sorrowful but relieved. There was a serenity and acceptance about her that was almost supernatural.

We had called Dr. John in Galesburg when death seemed imminent. He knew that everything possible was being done, so he decided not to come. He did want to have a post-mortem examination performed. I made all the arrangements, but could not get a pathologist to come out to perform it. I called Dr. John and told him about my problem. He hesitated a moment and said, "Then I shall do it myself. I must have those brain tissues because the disease was somewhat different in Henk than in Elsie. I want to see if there is a difference in damage to the cerebellum."

I met him at the airport that afternoon and took him to the funeral parlor. There I waited until he was finished with the autopsy.

"I'm not coming to the funeral," he said. "I'm afraid the family won't understand how I can perform an autopsy on someone I knew so well, and I don't want to face them now."

I took him back to the airport. I never discussed the matter with anyone—there were too many emotional factors involved, and I wanted to forget it.

Henk was buried only a few rods from his brother Bert, his sister Alice, and my sister Elsie. He had lived with ataxia fifteen years.

Now Aunt Artie was alone in her home. Her daughter Wilmena was now severely handicapped and living with her husband and two adopted daughters in Michigan. One of my cousins on my mother's side was helping her with the housework. Aunt Artie could visit Wilmena and her family, but the pleasure she received from seeing them was reduced by seeing her daughter following the same tragic course she had seen in three of her other children.

Wilmena was more affected in her throat and diaphragm, and she had great difficulty with coughing. I did not see her except on the occasional visits she and her family made to our community. I noted a rather rapid progress of the disease as compared to her brother Henk. From previous experience we could predict that she would not live as long as Henk, and death could come suddenly if she would contract pneumonia or even a bad cold.

These predictions came true all too soon. Three months after Henk's death we received the news that Wilmena had gone to be with her Lord. She had reached the age of thirty-six years and had never lost her charm and winning smile. She was loved by all who knew her, and tributes to her love and faithfulness as a pastor's wife poured into the sorrow-filled home.

Wilmena's body was laid to rest beside her brother Henk in Lakeview Cemetery. Thus Aunt Artie ended forty years of living with ataxia. Her husband and four of her five children had been sentenced to only ten years to live and she had lived, suffered, and wept with all of them.

17

Had God Answered Our Prayers?

Cousin Jim was now the only one left of Aunt Artie's family. He was nearly forty years old and in perfect health. The Lord had blessed his ministry in the churches he had served as pastor. His staunch faith in God and his ability to share it inspired all of us. The faith and assurance that his mother possessed never ceased to amaze him and no doubt was a major source of his own courage.

Jim and I spent some time talking and visiting after Wilmena's funeral. We reminisced about the many events that had happened since we had gone to Central College together some twenty-one years before.

"Henry," he said, "you and I and many others have spent hours and hours praying that God might reveal a cure for ataxia. Do you realize that as far as my family is concerned He has answered that prayer?"

"What do you mean?" I asked.

"Well," he replied, "not one of our family had children of their own, so the defective gene was not passed on to anyone. The disease is now eliminated in our immediate family, at least, and in that sense of the word it is cured. It really wasn't cured in the way we prayed it would be, but God answered our prayer in His own way. Isn't that the way God works at times?"

"Yes, I suppose you could consider that an answer to

prayer," I replied, "but for Dr. John and brother Bill that is small comfort."

"That's true, of course. But we've got to look into the future. The only realistic way to eliminate the disease is not to reproduce. We've got to continue to promote that idea among the dozens of our relatives who are still at risk."

"That's a harsh prescription, and I know not everybody will buy it."

"What's the alternative? One look at my mother's life should convince anyone that it's better than any other solution."

"Yes, at the present time I guess there's no other way. Dr. John has been advocating that all his life. But it's difficult for me to campaign for it when Hazel and I have six children of our own."

"That doesn't change the facts, and it doesn't mean we shouldn't advocate it. We have two adopted daughters, and so did Wilmena and her husband. I can assure you that the girls mean as much to us as if they were our own. It's the alternative my wife and I chose. Even though I now know that I could have had children of my own without passing the defective gene on to them, I have no regrets."

"But," I said, "I know that we must still continue to search for a cure. Both Dr. John and Bill could still be helped, as well as Bill's son. There may be thousands of others yet unborn, because it will be impossible to sell the idea of childlessness to everybody. I believe there is a cure and it may be a simple one; but until we find it, I know you are right. We have only one way to conquer it. And I will have to support it."

Brother Bill was now thirty-three, and the disease seemed to be progressing more rapidly in him than it was in Dr. John. He and his wife were making a good living in farming, but we all knew that in a matter of a few years he would not be able to function.

Bill was not an outspoken person, and he seldom revealed his feelings about anything. Dr. John tried to persuade him to try different medicines, but his reply usually was, "What's the use? Nothing helps anyway."

One day he drove his tractor over a hump of straw and became stuck on it. Suddenly the hot muffler of the tractor started the straw on fire, and within minutes the tractor was engulfed in flames. Bill stumbled through the fire and managed to escape unhurt, but the tractor was extensively damaged.

The accident indicated that operating a farm was dangerous for Bill, but he was persistent and refused to quit. Yet the time did come when he was forced to sell his livestock and some of his machinery. For a time he and his wife spent their winters in a warmer climate, believing that escaping from cold weather would help him avoid colds.

Slowly on the disease began to affect his whole personality. Instead of being a light-hearted, witty person, he became morose and somewhat bitter. Eventually he became very ill, and it was decided to transfer him to the Veteran's Hospital in Minneapolis. As we half-carried him to the car I noticed an almost complete resignation to his fate. He didn't seem to care about anything.

"Come now, Bill," I urged. "You'll need a stiff upper lip and some fight if you are to get well."

He turned around and stared at me for a moment.

"Why?" he asked.

I couldn't answer him.

At the hospital he was given good care, but pneumonia had set in. It became a fight for life—a fight he did not possess. A few days later the phone rang and it was Bill's wife. She had received a call from the hospital, she said, telling her that Bill was in critical condition, and could we take her to the hospital?

"Yes," I said. "I'll call Mom and let her know. Then Hazel

and I will pick you up and we'll get there as fast as we can."

My mother was now seventy-nine years old and not very well. Any tension might cause her to become ill, so we decided it was best for her not to go.

The hospital was located directly across the city from us, and there were at least thirty traffic lights on the way. Providence directed our way; we hit every light green and found a parking place close to the entrance. We walked quickly to Bill's room. He was alive, but seemed to be in a semiconscious state. We recognized the signs of approaching death—his breathing was shallow and stopped at times. Shortly afterward Bill left his diseased body behind to be with the Lord. He knew of no reason for living, and I had no doubt in my mind that he had prayed to be released from a body that had become his prison. He had spent thirty-eight years on earth, with nearly ten of them in a handicapped condition.

We told Mom about Bill's death when we returned home. She had expected the news and had spent much time in prayer. She hung onto me as I told her that Bill had not suffered the last few hours and had quietly slipped away.

"Thank God for that," she said.

Bill was buried near Pa and Elsie. As we laid his body to rest, I realized that out of the twelve Schut cousins who all had the same grandparents, six had died of ataxia. Of the fifty-two first cousins on my father's side, thirty-eight had been "at risk." Of these, nineteen had become afflicted. Eighteen had died, and now Dr. John was the only one left who had the disease and was still living. Besides him, my brother Bert J., my cousins Jim and Harold, and myself were the only Schut-Mol cousins still alive.

It was heartrending to see Dr. John trying to stand beside the grave. Holding on to me and his wife, he looked down at Bill's casket and slowly stammered, "Now I'm the only one left for us to fight for."

18

"I'm Not Licked Yet"

It had been difficult for John to see Bill lose the will to live. They were brothers, but their philosophy of life and attitude toward ataxia could hardly be more different. I had lived with each one long enough to know their personal relationship to God and how they felt concerning His control of events on earth.

Dr. John believed that he was forgiven for his sins through faith that Jesus Christ had died for him. He believed that God was great and powerful and that He provided for people both physically and spiritually. But he also believed that most of life's events were determined by mankind's own actions. He steadfastly maintained that a cure for ataxia could be found only by research and hard work.

Bill also believed that his salvation and eternal destiny depended on his acceptance of Jesus Christ as his Savior; but he believed, in addition, that the sovereign grace and will of God determined nearly all of the events in a person's life. I'm sure that he was not always happy with how God had planned his life, but his belief that God makes no mistakes and that He does all things for the good of those who love Him gave Bill a measure of serenity and peace. He felt that death was an event that could not be postponed, regardless of the efforts that were made to maintain life.

Dr. John stayed in Galesburg for only a little more than a year. He established a private practice in Anoka, Minnesota, and was quite successful there. But after only a few years he could no longer walk alone and had to give up the practice. Yet he vowed never to give up the fight to lick the disease that plagued his body. This determination seemed to deter the progress of the disease.

Dr. John's will to live and his efforts to find a cure for ataxia were the central emphases in his life. He had been active in research in Washington, D.C.; Anoka, Minnesota; Galesburg, Illinois; and the University of Minnesota. Despite this, he was frustrated because he had never had the opportunity to devote full time to this purpose. So he sought the means and opportunity to initiate a more intensive program. In 1957, about four years before Bill died, he attracted a group of men and women who were willing to support a small venture in this direction. Dr. John knew that he would soon be forced to quit his medical practice, but he thought he could still direct research from a wheelchair. That year Dr. John, I, and several other interested persons organized the National Ataxia Foundation. The Glenwood Hills Hospital of Minneapolis graciously donated the space and much of the laboratory material. Dr. John was elated.

But research takes money, and we had very little to start with. The first thing we had to do was to raise funds so Dr. John could establish and operate his research. We tried door-to-door solicitation, but most of the time we were met with a blank stare and the question, "Ataxia! What's that? Never heard of it."

It seemed that educating the public about ataxia would be our first task. In communities where members of our family lived it was well known, but most communities had never heard of it.

Mrs. Julia Schuur, a daughter of one of my cousins, now entered the scene. She had traveled with Dr. John while he was making the film on ataxia in 1948, and the tragic plight of ataxia victims had made an indelible impression on her mind and heart. At the time a dynamic young student, she vowed that when the time came she would donate as much time and effort as she could to support the fight against ataxia. (Julia's grandmother was my Aunt Carrie. Her mother, Ethel De Kraai Sankey, had escaped the disease so Julia was not facing the possibility of becoming afflicted.)

Dr. John said, "I know what we ought to do. If we can get the film I produced while I was in the army, we can show that to different organizations. That will teach the public about ataxia."

"That's where I fit in," said Julia. "I helped produce that film, and even though it's quite technical, I can explain it."

We sent for the film, had several copies made, and used it whenever we had the opportunity. Julia was successful in getting a limited amount of funds in this manner. Other persons and I used the film for this purpose also, but it was a tedious and time-consuming process. Besides, we all had our own work to do. Consequently much of the correspondence and fund-raising had to be done by Dr. John and his wife, Mary.

Dr. John once said, "I spend so much time raising funds I don't have time to work on my research. It's so frustrating. Can't you take more time off?"

"Asking people for money is just not my line," I answered. "I'm willing to help in other ways, but I must make a living for my family."

"I think you ought to drop everything and help me. Then when I find a cure I can pay you back," he insisted.

"If I were certain you could find a cure soon I might consider it, but I can't jeopardize my family's future."

We soon found another way in which I could help.

"I've received a small grant from the government to do some blood linkage studies," said John one day. "The rationale is that there may be a certain blood type or a substance in the blood that is characteristic of ataxia victims. I need blood samples from as many ataxia victims as I can get, as well as from their brothers and sisters who did not become affected. I can run tests on the blood to determine if there is a difference between the blood of the victims and the blood of their normal brothers or sisters."

"That sounds interesting," I replied. "What can I do?"

"First you must find the patients. Then you can find a good nurse to go with you to do the actual blood drawing."

"That I will do. One of our cousins is a nurse, and I'm sure she will take time off to help me."

"Fine. I'll plan on that."

I wrote people who had ataxia in their families, many of whom lived in different areas of the country. I asked them to meet in central locations so we would not have to travel to every home.

We had good cooperation. We were able to collect blood from many victims, from others who were at risk, and from healthy persons who were past the age of onset.

The studies performed on these blood samples were published, but no significant differences were found. So we had explored another blind alley.

One day John said in desperation, "Henry, I've got an idea. I want to exchange two pints of blood with you. We have the same type, so there won't be a reaction. I'm wondering if you would show temporary symptoms of ataxia. I'm sure your body would restore any damage if we didn't do it too often. I'd like to know if your blood would affect the ataxia in my body."

"I'll give you some of mine," I said, "but I can't take the chance of taking yours. Your blood might trigger a process that can't be stopped."

"Then I'm going to try to get periodic blood transfusions just to see what happens."

So he made arrangements to receive blood transfusions from the Minneapolis blood bank. He continued to get them until he was certain they had no value.

Julia Schuur, in the meantime, had aroused some interest and obtained some funds in communities surrounding her home where ataxia was known. Soon we were able to purchase several pieces of research equipment.

One of the machines was able to determine and measure the different chemicals in urine, spinal fluid, and other body fluids. It was a lengthy and intricate process. The results then were tabulated, recorded, and (most important of all) interpreted. This last part was Dr. John's job. Here I could detect a deterioration of his thinking ability. I noted that he could not keep the information organized in his mind, and that he sometimes failed to interpret similar results in the same way. But he was persistent. He constantly tested his own urine, comparing it with that of anyone in the hospital who was willing to supply a sample.

His disposition did not improve. In fact, he became more difficult than ever to live with, and he had trouble keeping lab workers. He even began to have mental delusions. He would say, "I'm sure my assistant is planning to poison me."

"That's not so," I would exclaim. "Why should he want to do that? He would be out of a job if he did."

"That may be true, but some fishy things are happening around here and I don't trust him."

"Aw, forget it," I told him, "and use your head for a better purpose."

He would then abruptly change the subject.

Another of Dr. John's projects was obtaining a strain of mice who had a form of ataxia. "I'm going to have them reproduce," he said, "and find the genetic pattern in each generation. I'll also study the brains of those that have ataxia at different stages of the disease and see if I can discover anything significant. I've ordered some cages, and we will take down every detail of the studies."

At first Dr. John came in from his home to work in the lab, but as his handicaps became more severe it was decided to have him remain in the hospital near his lab. He was now collecting disability insurance and was able to pay the special room rate the hospital charged him.

The problems of ataxia in our relatives did not go unnoticed by our children. How could they? Uncles, aunts, and cousins were dying of a disease other people did not have. And although our children were not at risk at any time, the stigma of the disease was to some extent transferred to them. Only after a lengthy explanation by a doctor would some people accept the fact that our children could not get it, and even then some remained doubtful.

Our oldest son, Lawrence, was blessed with a scientific mind, and no conversation about ataxia escaped his attention. When Lawrence was in high school Dr. John often remarked, "Lawrence, you should become a doctor too. Then you can continue my work if I don't live long enough to complete it."

The words met a receptive ear. After completing high school in 1954 Lawrence entered a premed course at Hope College in Holland, Michigan, and in 1958 he entered the University of Minnesota Medical College. Dr. John was elated. He couldn't wait to get Lawrence started on ataxia research. But medical school did not leave much time for research so Dr. John had to employ patience—a trait which was not his particular gift.

When brother Bill died in 1961, Lawrence was in his third year of medical school. Wayne, our second son, was in his last year at Central College. Our four daughters, Marilyn, Darlene, Linda, and Lois were in senior and junior high school.

Aunt Artie had been spending the summers in her home in Silver Creek and the winters with her son Jim in Michigan. She was seventy-six years old, and her body was beginning to show the years of struggle. In January of 1962 she began to have health problems, which slowly became so severe that she was taken to the hospital. Confused by drugs and her age, she was injured by a fall from her hospital bed. Jim and his family came from Michigan to see her. She rallied for a short time and Jim returned home. But her body was worn out. Ever so slowly she drifted toward death. On February 16, 1962, my Uncle Arnold Vandergon and I held her hands as she crossed the great divide. It was a fitting climax to a lifetime of grief and sorrow. Her struggles were over, but her influence on my life and the lives of hundreds of others will go on. She was buried beside Uncle Will, who had already been with his Savior for forty-four years.

We had prospered in our farming operation, but I was not convinced that I wanted to work on the farm for the rest of my life. Hazel and I also knew that neither one of our two sons wanted to farm, so we began to consider some alternatives. I was too old to become a doctor, but there was a great need for teachers. After much prayer and thinking I asked Hazel if she would support my idea of returning to college.

"I know you have never given up that idea," she said. "I'm with you all the way."

I started my third attempt to get an education in 1960, when I was forty-nine years old. I enrolled in St. Cloud State College to obtain a major in mathematics and science. The going was rough after being out of school for twenty-six years. I had some chores to do in the morning and evening, and I commuted twenty-three miles. We were able to keep our farm employee for the first two years. The last year we sold our livestock, and I worked the farm until I graduated in December of 1963.

After teaching one year in Upsala, Minnesota, I secured a position teaching junior high mathematics in my hometown of Maple Lake.

During these years Dr. John was able to continue his research sporadically, but without really accomplishing very much. He could no longer use his hands to work with chemicals or to write. Mary and her parents visited him faithfully and helped him in every way they could. Finally the hospital staff decided that the space being occupied by the lab was needed for other purposes. It was a bitter development for Dr. John. We wanted to sell the research equipment, but Dr. John refused.

"Maybe Lawrence can use it when he completes medical school," he said.

"I'm afraid it will be obsolete by that time," I replied. "In fact, I checked with the hospital and there are only a few things that have any value anymore. Research techniques are changing so rapidly that the machines you're using have been replaced with better ones."

"I won't let you sell them, nor will I let you destroy those mice. I worked years on them and I can still learn from them," he replied.

We were able to find a storage room for the equipment and a small room for the cages of mice. John had someone wheel him over to the mice every day, where he checked those who had young ones and tried to predict which ones of the litter would get ataxia. He had hoped to produce a strain of mice that was 100 percent ataxic, but that was not possible as most of the diseased mice died before they could reproduce.

Lawrence graduated from medical school and decided to continue his education in the field of neurology. Dr. John helped him financially and gave him the impetus to go further in his chosen specialty. He felt, in a way, that he could live on in his nephew.

"I didn't find a cure," he said, "but I hope Lawrence can. Maybe even soon enough to cure me. I ain't dead yet!"

One morning I was called out of my classroom for a telephone call. I was told to hurry to my mother's home. Hazel was already there. My Aunt Bertha, who was visiting with Mom at the time, met me at the door. She was crying.

"What's happened?" I asked.

"Your mother passed away just a short time ago. She got up this morning, started to dress, and said, 'I don't feel very well.' Then she fell back on the bed, gasped a few times, and was gone."

I walked to the bedroom and there she lay as peacefully as if she were asleep.

When we told John, all he could say was, "Poor Ma, poor Ma."

Really, she needed no pity now. Dr. John was the one who needed pity. She had lived a full life of eighty-two years with a childlike faith that I was never able to comprehend fully—but which I had learned to appreciate very much. She left a legacy to our family that could not be measured in dollars.

We laid her to rest beside Pa, who had been buried there forty-two years earlier. Now she was united with him and with Bill and Elsie.

19

Why Does He Want to Live?

After being in the hospital for six years, working in his research lab during the day and at times into the night, Dr. John had to make a decision. His disability insurance had run out. His personal finances were inadequate to sustain him in the hospital, even at reduced rates. He had hoped that the National Ataxia Foundation would be able to continue funding the research and perhaps even support him and others who were afflicted. But adequate funds did not come in.

Dr. John was a veteran and could choose to go to the Veteran's Hospital in Minneapolis or return home to his wife, who was now living with her parents. Mary and her mother, Mart, would not consider taking him to the Veteran's Hospital, so arrangements were made to take him home.

No one knew how long Dr. John would live. He had already lived sixteen years since the memorable time his coffee cup slipped on his tray. This was six years beyond the expected ten years to live.

He had had one bout with pneumonia and had nearly choked to death, but by the quick action of the doctors a tracheotomy had been performed and he was able to breathe through a tube. The hole into his trachea was in his neck just below his Adam's apple. This was also used as a means of aspirating food or fluid from the lungs whenever the food did not follow the path to the stomach. To prevent infections, his lungs had to be rinsed out with an antiseptic every time they were aspirated. This was done with a plastic tube inserted through the hole in his throat and pushed deep into his lungs. That triggered his cough reflex. His whole body doubled up. He flailed his hands as he tried to cough but couldn't. It was terrible to see. Fortunately, Mary and Mart learned to perform the task quickly.

Dr. John was now almost completely helpless. He spent much of his time watching television, more to escape the problems of ataxia than for entertainment. He became difficult to understand, and Mary and Mart did their best to translate the noises he made. Yet he always flashed a big smile at Hazel and me when we called.

For Mart, Dr. John's mother-in-law, life became a routine of feeding, nursing, pleading, listening, and watching. She carried the greatest burden of his care since Mary had to go to work to support the family. Because Mary needed her rest at night, Mart had trained herself to wake up at the slightest hint of trouble in the room next to hers.

I had seen the care and concern Aunt Artie and Mom had had for their children, but never have I seen the kind of love, care, and devotion that Mart had for her son-in-law.

A visit to John was not a pleasant experience. As the disease progressed, different muscles became affected one by one. In time the small muscle that was supposed to close the entrance to the trachea when he swallowed food or liquid did not work at all. Much of the food went directly into his lungs and had to be suctioned out with the aspirator. Frequently he turned blue as the lungs were not able to get enough oxygen.

For him to eat, it finally became necessary to insert a collapsed balloon into the trachea through the hole in his throat. This then was inflated to close up the trachea below the hole and prevent food from entering the lungs. After he had eaten his meal the balloon was deflated and removed. Usually there was some food left in the trachea just above the balloon. This had to be rinsed out and aspirated. The last two years of his life he could not eat or drink anything without having this balloon in place.

One of his most frustrating experiences in the last years of his life was trying to communicate with others. When we could not understand him he often pounded the bed in anger and frustration. We frequently resorted to questions which he could answer Yes or No.

In 1971, ill with pneumonia, he was taken to the hospital. He was blue when he arrived there, but quick administration of oxygen revived him. A roomful of machinery and several antibiotics kept him alive, and after several weeks he was able to return home.

After this bout with pneumonia there were times when he didn't seem to recognize me. It was impossible to tell if this was because his sight and hearing were poor, because he was angry and refused to answer, or because he was only semiconscious. But even in his semiconscious state his determinaton to live kept him alive.

In January of 1972, he was again afflicted with pneumonia. Our son Lawrence, now a neurologist, was called— as he usually was when Dr. john became ill. I could not go to his bedside, as I was recovering from a slight heart attack and had been instructed to stay away from all situations of stress.

"Why don't you let him die at home?" I asked Lawrence.

"I can't," he answered. "Uncle John made me promise years ago that I would fight to the last breath to keep him alive, and I must keep that promise."

Why anyone would want to live in a body that was so helpless I could not understand.

So he was again put into a room full of machines. He

never regained consciousness. I did go to see him briefly, but saw only a body that weighed eighty pounds and was breathing by machine. Ever so slowly life ebbed away as his spirit fought to the last. On February 17, 1972, the fight ceased.

He was fifty-one years old and had lived with ataxia for twenty-three years, longer than anyone else of our family. He had out-fought and out-lived all of his similarly afflicted cousins. He had dedicated his life to the task of curing ataxia, but had to leave this world with the task unfinshed, the cure undiscovered.

We laid him to rest beside Elsie. Nineteen years earlier he had said, "That leaves one for me, but I'm going to fight to the last breath to stay out of it. You can bet on that!"

He had kept his word.

Mary had asked that the funeral service be led by Cousin Jim. He came from Michigan to conduct the service. It was a fitting climax to the lives and deaths of all of our cousins who had to die a little everyday for ten or more years.

The sermon is included here with his permission.

This is hardly a time for grieving, though from a human standpoint it might be. Indeed if I linger too long at the crossroads of reflections and memory, I find myself only a few feet away from an outburst of tears. But this is also a time of triumph. The struggle is over. John is no longer the victim of the malady he has fought so long. In that context I find myself only *inches* away from joining the chorus of those who sing, "Praise the Lord."

The thing I want to remember most about John is what occurred when I called on him a year or two ago. Already the weakening of his body had deprived him of the normal means of communication, but he was still alert. He knew that I was there and I felt he knew what I was saying. In the course of the visit I leaned over him and said, "John, in whom do you put your trust? Is Jesus Christ your Lord and Savior?"

Unable to respond in words, he responded affirmatively with a light in his face and a groan so characteristic of those who have been so afflicted.

I want to speak a word of consolation and commendation. As to consolation, it's not all that easy for me, for I find myself in the midst of all those who need it. But I want to say this: May God who has brought our lives into being and manages them to their completeness give you the peace that comes to those who trust in Him.

As to the word of commendation, I want to speak directly to you, Mary, and to your parents. The kind of love, understanding, and care that you gave to John during those long days and years of pain, agony, and struggle, finds a parallel in that which our Lord Himself did during the years of His earthly ministry. Few of us will ever be able to understand the extent of your dedication to John. And we thank God for you.

John will be missed. There will be an emptiness. Lest you fill that void with something that is meaningless and irrelevant, I want to plead with you that you fill it with the love of Christ. Drive yourself often to your knees. Come often to the reading of the Word of God, the Bible. In short, find Jesus Christ to be your hope and stay.

When I was first told that John's passing was imminent and that I would be here this morning, I began the search for a passage of Scripture from which to speak. For a time I considered Philippians the first chapter, the twenty-first verse. In the Revised Standard Version it reads like this: "For to me to live is Christ, and to die is gain." The text became remarkably fresh to me as I read it in the Living Bible: "For to me, living means opportunities for Christ, and dying— well, that's better yet." The text was used by Rev. Adelphos Dykstra at my brother Bert's funeral nearly thirty-three years ago. I've never forgotten it, and I thought it might be fitting again. But a little later another text came to my mind, the one from the apostle Paul, where he alludes to suffering and says, "For I reckon that the sufferings of this present time are not worthy to be compared with the glory which shall be revealed in us" (Romans 8:18, AV).

I worked with that text a little while. Then one morning I was alerted from sleep at about four or five o'clock. A text flashed before my mind's eye. I couldn't quote it verbatim at the time, but the substance of it was there as though the Spirit was shaming me for not knowing it word for word. He seemed to say to me "I've given you enough; go now and look it up."

Some time later I found it in John 13 where there is an account of our Lord washing the disciples' feet. After Simon Peter objected to what Jesus was doing the Lord said, "What I am doing you do not know now, but afterward you will understand" (John 13:7, RSV).

The Living Bible translates it as follows: "You don't understand now why I am doing it; some day you will."

There are two thoughts that come to me from these words. The first is this: *God is doing something.*

From the passage of Scripture we learn that it was the night before the cross. The supper having been served, Jesus Christ rose, girded Himself with a towel, poured some water into a basin, and of all things began to wash the disciples' feet. It was a very difficult thing for Peter to accept. One can almost feel the vibrations of rejection in his soul as he objected to what our Lord was doing. It was as though Peter was saying, "Master, don't let those clean white hands touch my smelly feet."

To which Jesus replied, "Peter, you don't understand why I am doing this, but let me tell you this—I am doing *something*."

We learn later on in the chapter that our Lord intended to use this as an example for the disciples. Just as He was willing to stoop down and become a servant, so they were to stoop down and become servants too. It is essential for us to understand this truth if we are going to live meaningful and expressive lives. We encounter much doubt, frustration, and disbelief because we don't understand this.

Think of the problems of our day: hunger, pollution, racial injustice, and a hundred more. What a difference it would make if we could see God working out His eternal plan through them!

Think of the affliction that has brought low so many of our loved ones in the prime of their lives. It is easy for us to object. It isn't even difficult to become bitter and to suggest that God is unfair and unjust.

But it is a thousand times more satisfying—and honest, if you will—to regard these as experiences through which God is working out His will and bringing His truth to light. I do not know what it is all about, but the one thing I *do* know (and all that I need to know) is that *God is doing something!*

The second thing that comes to my mind from this text is this: *some day He is going to show us what it is!*

Peter's impetuousness at the feet-washing scene is both interesting and revealing. Peter complains that the thing ought to be turned around; he and the other disciples should be washing Jesus' feet. But Jesus Christ turns to him and says, "Peter, don't interfere with me. I'm doing *something*. I'm not ready yet to pull the curtain and let you know what is really going on. But as for now, Peter, get off my back. Sit down in the reserved seat I have prepared for you and just watch the stage. Wait for me to pull the curtain. In time I will show you what it is all about."

Now, it is essential, if we are to know the satisfied life, that we learn the truth of this. We don't *need* to know everything. It is enough to know that He is doing *something*. What really matters is that we have the faith to hold out until the day when He will show us everything.

I've often thought that one of the first things I will do when I see my Savior face to face is to ask Him, "Lord, why did You do these things to us?" I don't intend to ask it out of bitterness but out of great expectancy. I will say to Him, "Show me, Lord, the glory of it." I have the faith to believe that when He draws the curtain back and shows me the total performance, it will be unbelievably *good!*

We must remember, of course, that if we are to behold the glory of it all we must know Him as our very own. The supreme question of the hour is not, "Lord, why have you been doing this?" but "What have you done with Jesus Christ?" I address that question to every one of us.

We leave now for the final resting place. We go there, not in fear or despair, but in hope. God is doing *something*. While we see now only a fraction of the whole, someday we will see it all. Praise be to God! Amen.

20
God Leads His Dear Children Along

Dr. John's death was, in a sense, the end of an era. He was the last of my near relatives to die from ataxia. As I look back over the fifty or more years I wept and prayed with and for them, I sometimes wonder if it may turn out to have been a long, tragedy-filled dream.

Thoughts, dreams, events, and heartaches all seem to clamor for expression in words—words that I cannot find; words that will never fully transmit to the reader the feelings of my heart.

There are words of gratitude. I am grateful to God for sparing me and my family from the ravages of ataxia. I am grateful to Hazel for marrying me in spite of the risk of living with an invalid for ten years, for caring for our family when I was called to the bedside of my loved ones, and for sharing my burden of sorrow.

I thank God for six children who have shown in many concrete ways that they love us. I am thankful that they have demonstrated by their lives a concern for those who are less fortunate than they. I thank God for their realization that good health and brilliant minds are gifts of God to be used wisely and lovingly.

God has taught us through the years that happiness can be found in spite of tragedy. He taught us that to have contentment our dreams do not need to be fulfilled. He taught us that faith can become stronger in the midst of sorrow. He taught us to trust Him for each tomorrow when we dared not make plans beyond today. He taught us that our family was not the only one that cried out, "Why me, O Lord?" He taught us to have compassion for the heartbroken and how to give comfort to the sorrowing.

And who could imagine that the tragedy in our family would be used by God to bring happiness into the lives of others? That He did just that was brought home to me by Cousin Jim. He said, "Do you know what our two adopted daughters, Judy and Barbara, told us some time ago? They said, 'Dad, in a way we are glad you had ataxia in your family, because if you hadn't you would probably have had children of your own and you wouldn't have adopted us.'"

As I look back over the years I find that God used each passing experience as a chisel by which He molded and fashioned me into an instrument He could use. I wanted to become a doctor or perhaps a medical missionary, but He closed every door to these professions. I wanted to leave my home community of Silver Creek, but He tied me down with responsibilities in my home from which I could not escape. I wanted to study medicine, but He opened the barn door and told me to milk cows. Then when He thought the time was right He helped me to become a teacher.

I realize now that if I had continued to go to college and medical school I would have become an M.D. just when World War II began and would no doubt have been drafted immediately into the armed forces. I doubt if my pathway would ever have led back to Silver Creek.

I do not know exactly why God led me in the path I have

traveled. Perhaps it was because He wanted me to support my loved ones when they needed it so much. Perhaps He knew that my questioning mind would not be able to maintain faith under the onslaught of a scientific education.

I know I needed to see Aunt Artie on her knees beside her bed. I needed to hear a sister say, "Whatever God wills is good." I needed the inspiration of a mother who wrote on her Bible bookmark, "Be still and know that I am God."

I do not know why so many people must suffer in this life. But I do know that pain, tragedy, and distress need not cause us to lose our faith in an ever-loving God.

As Peter could not understand why Jesus washed his feet, I cannot understand why the millions of prayers from suffering humanity seem to bring so few results.

The answer Jesus gave to Peter comes ringing across the centuries: "What I am doing you do not know now, but afterward you will understand" (John 13:7, RSV). I am positive that when the door to eternity swings open I will see clearly the goal to which God has led His dear children along.

Thousands out there are still hurt and bitter. Many cry out in frustration and anger, "Why me, O Lord?" The task of finding a cure for many diseases has just begun. Yet we look into a future with confident faith that sometime, somehow, God will pull back the cover and say, "Here it is!"

We must learn, too, that death is not a monster to be feared. With faith in God we can approach it courageously. Perhaps a time may come when we can even welcome it. In reality we all start dying the moment we are born. Our family was different only in the sense that ataxia forced us to come to terms with that reality earlier and more vividly. Through the eyes of loved ones like my father, some of us caught a premature glimpse of the beautiful city that lies just beyond the door of death.

"An illusion," you say. "A figment of the imagination."

Not for me! It's as real as this book. I have seen hope when there was no reason for hope. I have seen faith that conquers the agony of a living death. I have experienced the promise "that neither death, nor life, nor angels, nor principalities, nor things present, nor things to come, nor powers, nor height, nor depth, nor anything else in all creation, will be able to separate us from the love of God in Christ Jesus our Lord" (Romans 8:38-39, RSV).

Isn't that great!

Epilogue

When the National Ataxia Foundation was established in 1957, the disease of ataxia was hardly known except in medical literature and by the families which suffered from it. Even in their own communities the presence of the disease was a "secret"—discussed privately by the neighbors but seldom publicly acknowledged by the affected families.

That situation occurred even more often in "the old country." In the summer of 1972, Hazel and I spent three weeks in the Netherlands tracing down some of the descendants of my great-grandfather, Gerrit Jan Vanden Berg. We were successful in finding a number of people there who had the disease, but we were asked not to publicize any names. Even the doctor who was treating one of the families asked that his name be kept secret.

Hopefully, that situation is changing.

In 1971, the Associated Press carried a long article about ataxia in our family. Hundreds of letters poured into the mail boxes of the afflicted families and to the office of the National Ataxia Foundation. The letters told of thousands of others who were either seeking help and information or who were offering to help us in the struggle against ataxia.

An article in the *Ladies Home Journal* of September 1973 is entitled "The Family Secret." It tells how two house-

151

wives from Colton, South Dakota, "have braved tradition and disapproval of in-laws to expose 'the secret' "—"the secret" being the fact that both of their husbands, Vernon and Ken Swier, are victims of our family's ataxia.

In December 1976, the Ann Landers column published the address of the National Ataxia Foundation with the request that any readers affected by or interested in ataxia should write to the office for information and help. Nearly one thousand people responded from every state in the union and many from other countries. It is conservatively estimated that we have discovered three hundred more families who face the problems of ataxia.

Mental retardation was also once regarded as a disgrace, and its victims were kept out of sight. Thanks to men and women like the Hubert Humphreys and the Joseph Kennedys, mental retardation has been brought into the open. These people have shown that they are not ashamed of a loved one who has been born with a handicap. We hope that this attitude may come true for more and more families of ataxia victims.

The National Ataxia Foundation has grown considerably in recent years, and the interest in hereditary diseases has increased tremendously. Studies have shown that some other hereditary diseases can be diagnosed before birth, and efforts are being made to take corrective measures to give the baby a normal life. Whether this will ever be possible with hereditary ataxia is not known at this time.

Many avenues of research remain to be followed. The paths are intricate and long, but there is hope. The search for the initial factor that causes the degeneration of the nerve cells in the central nervous system continues throughout the world. In 1976, two new discoveries gave us some hope, even though they are still in the experimental stage today. A drug has been discovered that seems to affect ataxia in animals. Permission is being sought to try it on people.

Another area that is being explored is an electric relay mechanism that is implanted near the nerve center. This augments the nerve impulses, and the patient is able to function more effectively. But this mechanism does not arrest or cure the disease.

In the Schut-Vanden Berg family, ataxia is still taking its toll. It has infiltrated into at least twenty-six different families. There are at least fifty people who are at risk or have the disease. Heartache and sorrow are still very much a part of our clan.

Dr. Lawrence Schut spends a good share of his time working with and helping ataxia sufferers who come to him. I still spend much of my time working with the National Ataxia Foundation. Julia Schuur has played a very important part in making the Foundation a success. Many people from other families have now joined us. It is our hope that funds can be obtained from government and private sources to continue the fight against ataxia.

Many people are working without pay to help us. I have learned to know and love many of them. I wish I could express my gratitude to each one by name, but that is impossible.

The National Ataxia Foundation has been instrumental in lowering the incidence of ataxia by counseling people to use the only known method of eliminating ataxia—birth control. This is definitely not the most desirable solution, but right now it is the only alternative to giving children a probable sentence of "Only Ten Years to Live."

Those interested in receiving additional information can contact The National Ataxia Foundation at 4225 Golden Valley Road, Minneapolis, MN 55422; telephone (612) 521-2233.

Appendices

How Dominant Hereditary Ataxia Is Transmitted

Hereditary ataxia is passed from generation to generation through defective genes.

Each child born of a parent with dominant hereditary ataxia (also known as Marie's ataxia) has a 50-50 chance of getting ataxia. It is passed directly from parent to child. If the child does not develop ataxia his or her children in turn cannot become afflicted, and future generations are free of the disease. The symptoms usually appear around ages 20-40.

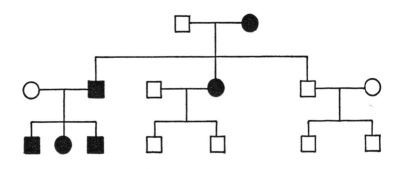

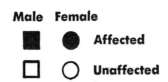

Male Female

■ ● Affected

□ ○ Unaffected

Genealogical Chart
of the
Vandenberg Family
(to 1946)

The following chart was made in 1946 and was current at that time; the size of the family tree had more than doubled by 1970.

I have chosen to identify only those who were or are closely associated with me, the author. My symbol can be found in Generation IV number 19. The '10 indicates the date of birth; the 4 in the diamond beneath indicates the four children we had by 1946.

Generation III number 5 was my father, John Schut, married to Jennie Mol; III number 7, my Uncle Henry Schut, married to Bertha Mol; III number 8 my Uncle Will Schut, married to Artie Mol.

Generation IV number 20, my brother Bert; IV number 21, sister Elsie; IV number 22, brother Dr. John; IV number 23, brother Bill; IV number 24, cousin Harold; IV number 25, cousin Wilbert; IV number 26, cousin Alice; IV number 27, cousin Bert W.; IV number 28, cousin Henry W.; IV number 29, cousin James; and IV number 30, cousin Wilmena.

I also write briefly about cousin Ed, IV number 16. As the reader can understand, the experiences of each family would fill a book and would differ from this story in many details; but the heartaches, differences of attitude, and symptoms of the disease would be essentially the same. Our common enemy caused us to keep in close contact even though we lived in various parts of the country. This pedigree is one of the largest to be found with a dominant, fatal, hereditary disease.

There are hundreds of hereditary diseases, mostly of the recessive type, but only a relatively few produce the heartache and problems to the entire family of the victims that hereditary ataxia does.

Genealogical chart of the Vandenberg family, pre-
pared by Dr. John W. Schut with the aid of the
author, 1946. The Schut involvement began in gen-
eration II when Allie Vandenberg (left side of the
chart) married Hendrick Schut and had nine chil-
dren, seven of whom got the disease (generation
III). The author is No. 19 of generation IV.

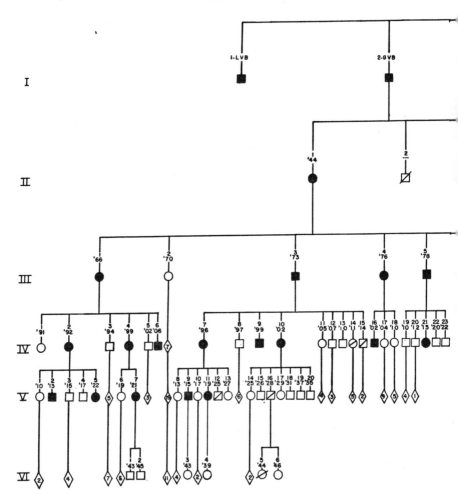

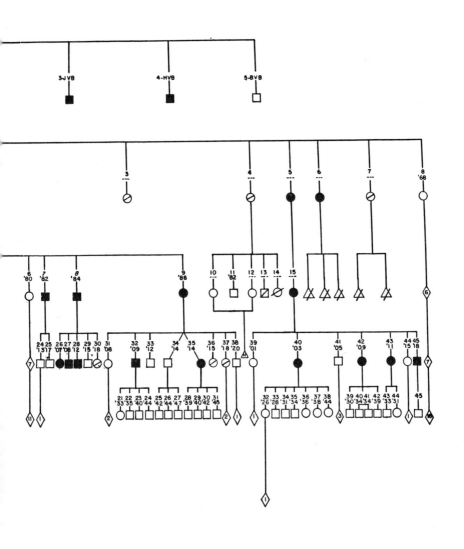

Male Female

■ ● Affected

□ ○ Unaffected

▲ Sex unknown
◆ Number of children born
   to non-ataxic members
◨ ⊘ Questionably affected individual
⧄ ◨ ⊘ Death in infancy, or in the
   pre-ataxic period

Genealogy No.	Age at Death, Yr.	Age at Onset, Yr.	Duration, Yr.
Male Parents			
II- 1	42	....	....
II- 4	40	....	....
II- 5	44	....	....
II- 6	32	....	....
IV- 7	33	21	12
IV- 9	47	25	22
IV-10	36	23	13
IV-14	..	34	....
IV-15	..	33	....
IV-21	..	26.5	....
IV-23	..	27	....
IV-26	37	25	12
IV-27	30	20	10
IV-28	..	30	....
IV-30	..	29.5	....
Average	38.0	26.7	13.8
S. D.	± 5.4	± 4.3	± 4.7
Female Parents			
III- 1	41.0	26.5	14.5
III- 3	42.0	30.5	11.5
III- 4	36	32	4.0
III- 5	46	37.5	8.5
III- 7	36	31	5.0
III- 8	34	21.5	12.5
III- 9	34	25.5	8.5
III-15	44	....	....
IV- 2	35	20	15.0
IV- 4	27	20	7.0
IV- 6	42	29.5	12.5
IV-16	40	25.5	14.5
IV-32	42	25	17.0
IV-35	..	28.5	....
IV-36	..	32.5	....
IV-43	..	31.5	....
IV-45	35	30	5.0
IV-46	32	31	1.0
IV-48	..	25	....
V- 2	31	22	9.0
V- 5	25	17	8.0
V- 7	..	25	....
V- 9	..	25	....
V-11	26	19	7.0
V-16	..	21	....
Average	36.0	26.3	9.4
S. D.	± 6.0	± 6.5	± 4.3

Comparison of age of onset and age of death in ataxia victims, compiled by Dr. John Schut, 1950.

Current Genealogical Chart of the Schut Family

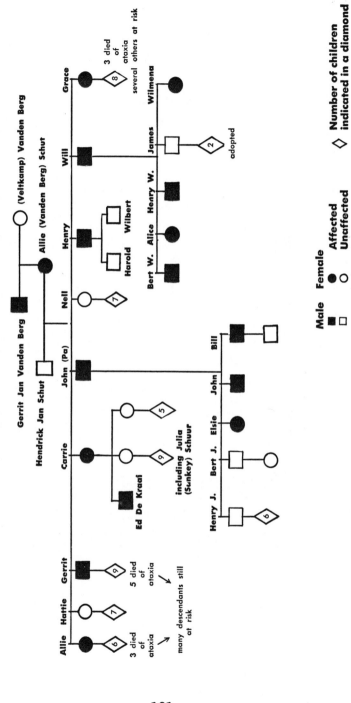

Current genealogical chart of the Schut family, with names of those mentioned in the book.

Handwriting Sample
of an
Ataxia Victim

Edgerton, Minn.
10/29/35.

Dear Doctor:

Rec'd your letter of Sept. 24, but have received no answer to my last letter of October. And so, I am undecided as to what to do. As it is over two hundred miles to Minneapolis, from here, I cannot, in my condition, make the trip to consult you when I would like to. You wrote in your last letter, that you had a new method of treatment, I am very anxious to try this, I cannot do anything but sit around and read or look wise(?), so a yes or no from you would be very welcome around here. I had hoped that it would not be necessary to take up any more of your time with my letters but — let us hope that, for the present at least, this is the last one. With best wishes, I remain

Sincerely yours

Ed De Kraai.

Sample of the handwriting of an ataxia victim, Ed De Kraai, 1935.